Happy Families

Patsy Collins

To my aunt Cherryl –
sorry for all the times I spelled your
name wrongly!

Contents

1. Money To Spend (Or Not)

Years ago, Sheila's Great Aunt Dylis won money on the football pools. Over a hundred pounds it had been, which at the time seemed an absolute fortune to the young Sheila.

"What will you spend it all on?" Sheila had asked.

Lots of other people had asked as well. Aunt Dylis had told them she'd use it to brighten rainy days. It was only with Sheila that she'd suggested anything specific.

"I might get a robot to do all my housework," she'd said. "That's what those scientists should be working on, not fake grass and trips to the moon. Who wants that?"

"Really? You're getting a robot? Like they have in Star Trek?" Sheila wasn't allowed to watch the show, but knew it featured clever things from the future.

"Maybe not. They always seem to go wrong or frighten people, from what I've heard."

"Then what will you buy, Aunty Dylis?"

"We'll have to think about it, Sheila love." She'd made a pot of tea and cut a home made walnut cake to help with that.

"I know what I'd spend it on," Sheila had said between mouthfuls. "A whole box of Milk Tray, just for me." The few times the family had enjoyed the luxury of a box of chocolates, her brother had grabbed Sheila's favourites without even looking to see what they were, and by the time their parents had taken a few, there weren't many left for

Sheila and her sister. Those few weren't divided evenly, or so it seemed to Sheila.

On her next visit, Aunt Dylis had asked her to nip down the shop and given her some money, including a whole pound note!

"What do you want me to fetch you, Aunty Dylis?"

"A box of chocolates, but you won't be eating them all, mind."

Sheila didn't mind sharing with her, especially as there were two layers so they could both sample every flavour. They'd done without cake that afternoon.

Next time the subject of Aunt Dylis's windfall came up, Sheila was again asked what she herself would use it for.

"My own copy of Jackie magazine." Her sister always managed to grab it first and sometimes circled the quiz answers, ripped out the pin ups or told her what happened in the story.

Great Aunt Dylis had given her the cover price. "You get the next issue as soon as it comes out and bring it round here, love."

Sheila had done just that. As it had been pouring with rain, Sheila had carried the magazine inside her coat and run all the way to Aunt Dylis's home. Her elderly relation enjoyed the bits Sheila read out and thought agony aunts Cathy and Claire generally gave good advice. Then they'd both done the quiz, with Great Aunt Dylis writing her answers on a piece of paper. Often instead of selecting A, B or C she made up her own funny ones.

The next time they'd had the conversation about Dylis's winnings, Sheila had suggested buying a pony.

Dylis had laughed. "And where would you keep that,

then?"

"I'd buy a field," Sheila replied without a moment's hesitation. "Don't ask me where I'd put that though!"

Sheila had laughed at her own joke. Of course she couldn't buy a pony, even if she really had what was left of Aunt Dylis's hundred pounds. As well as the field, she'd need a stable, saddle and food for it. Then there would be riding boots and hat for herself, plus riding lessons. That just wasn't going to happen.

A week later her dad had told her that a friend of his knew a farmer who owned horses. "Reckons he might let you ride if you help with mucking out and grooming them and all that."

An arrangement was made, allowing Sheila to spend as much of her free time with huge horses, and the farmer's children's adorable pony, as she liked. The children had grown too big for it, but were often persuaded to help Sheila climb on, lead her up and down the farm track, and offer advice. The animal was so placid she could soon manage to ride round the field without help.

Great Aunt Dylis offered to buy her a riding hat with part of her winnings, but that hadn't been necessary as Mum and Dad got her one for her birthday. Once she had that, Sheila was allowed to ride where she liked and had the next best thing to her own pony without spending even a ha'penny.

Gradually the plans about how to spend Aunt Dylis's money stopped featuring in the conversations the old lady shared with her great niece. They talked about other things; the farm, Sheila's first boyfriend and then her second boyfriend. Not much was said about the third.

Sheila assumed the money had long been spent. Luckily for her, despite Aunt Dylis's many plans for doing that, she'd actually left it in the Building Society to grow, right up until Sheila inherited it. As well as the money, there was a note saying, 'It's yours to do with as you like, but I suggest you use it to brighten a rainy day'.

The amount of Sheila's inheritance, although technically more than doubled, didn't seem such a massive sum as the initial winnings had done over a decade previously. It wasn't enough to change her life, but was enough to do something worthwhile with. Something interesting. Sheila was determined not to rush into spending it, despite the advice she was given.

"Put it towards a mortgage," her dad had suggested. Good advice no doubt, but it would be years before she'd be able to afford one and then it would be swallowed up and forgotten about.

"Get a car," was her brother's idea.

For a moment she imagined sitting behind the wheel of a stylish, open top sports car. That wouldn't be practical with her hair and the British weather. Nor was it realistic. Sheila might, just, have managed to buy something old and scruffy but she'd still have needed fuel and insurance and lessons.

"If it was me I'd blow it on something really pretty," her sister said. "Jewellery, maybe."

She was referring to her own legacy from Great Aunt Dylis; a gorgeous cat brooch with, they were almost sure, real diamonds for eyes. Sheila rarely went anywhere it would be appropriate to wear lavish jewellery and her sister was by then much better at sharing, so that idea wasn't given a great deal of consideration.

Sheila opened a special account for the money until she'd decided what to do with it. Then, using part of her wages, she bought herself a small box of Milk Tray and a magazine in Aunt Dylis's honour. She settled down to enjoy the sweet treat and some celebrity gossip. One of her favourite actresses had taken a cruise and the magazine featured several photographs. It looked so glamorous!

There was enough money in Sheila's account for a short cruise she thought. But not for the fancy evening dresses she'd want to wear, and the cocktails she'd want to sip and excursions to pyramids, temples and mountains. Not to mention presents for her family, including something extra nice for her sister as a thank you for the loan of the brooch. Better forget that idea then. Still, she would really like a holiday somewhere a bit more ordinary. The kind of place she could just wear the best of the clothes she had. Brighton perhaps, or Blackpool.

"Would you come with me?" she asked a work friend.

"Funny you should say that, I was going to ask you the same thing. Well, sort of."

"Oh?"

"My parents run a B&B, down in Margate. I'm looking after it for a week, so they can go away. It would be more fun with two of us and only half the work."

Her friend had taken care of the bathroom and bedrooms and Sheila cooked breakfasts and washed up. For most of the time though, they could see the sights, laze on the beach and dance the evenings away. The pair had shared other holidays since then, all of which they'd enjoyed, but it was that first one they most often recalled and laughed about when they met up. They'd had a brilliant time and it cost them little more than the train fare down, bottle of bronzing oil and rather a lot of ice cream.

As she hadn't had to pay for holiday accommodation, Sheila had enough money for some of those fancy dresses she'd fantasised about wearing. Not having any idea what might suit her and knowing she'd feel a little intimidated going into really posh shop put her off. Besides, where would she go in them?

Over the coming months and years, Sheila occasionally day dreamed about spending Aunt Dylis's legacy, but she never actually did. Once it was gone, the fun of the anticipation would be lost too. Perhaps that's why Dylis had kept hold of it? Sheila hoped that her own childish plans to spend it had added to her great Aunt's enjoyment of her winnings. Looking back at some of the mad things she'd suggested, that did seem likely.

The money remained in the account Sheila had set up for it, keeping pace with inflation and fuelling Sheila's imagination until the time came when she realised her other savings more than matched it. Even if she did decide what to spend it on, she'd no longer need her legacy for the purchase.

It wasn't until Sheila's teenage niece visited to show off her prom dress that Sheila made her decision. She was perhaps prompted by two things; it was a rainy day and the girl was wearing Great Aunt Dylis's cat brooch.

"Mum lent it to me. She said it will be mine one day, but not for a very long time, I hope."

That seemed likely. These days Sheila's sister read health magazines and only very occasionally indulged in a small bar of high quality dark chocolate.

"Did you know I was left money, by the person who gave your mum the brooch?"

"No! Was it loads?" her niece exclaimed.

"It seemed quite a lot back then and has been earning interest ever since."

"You haven't spent it? I would have."

"I still might, but if not I shall leave it to you."

"That's really nice of you, but I hope that too won't happen for a very long time."

"Don't worry, I intend to make you wait. But tell me, what will you spend it on once you have it?"

"Flying lessons," she said without hesitation. "Um, I don't suppose there will be enough for a plane?"

"I'm afraid not. Maybe a handsome instructor will fall in love with you and you can share his?"

"Obviously that would happen, but I've just met a lovely trainee electrician who's pretty much sweeping me off my feet and that's probably something which is better happening at ground level. Perhaps flying lessons wouldn't be such a good idea after all?"

"Maybe not," Sheila agreed.

"Never mind. As long as you look after yourself, I've got plenty of time to decide. I'll come up with something."

"I'm sure you will."

Actually Sheila wasn't entirely positive about that. She was even less sure when, over tea and cake, her niece said, "I know! I'll buy a couple of Angora rabbits. I could breed from them until I have enough to knit a mohair suit."

"But you can't knit!" Sheila had tried to teach her, but somehow they'd always ended up in a tangle of wool and fits of giggles.

The girl grinned. "Fair point, but I might get the hang of it one day."

No doubt she would have thought of something else before she'd got round to mastering the technique, if she ever did. Quite likely she'd change her mind many more times before she inherited Sheila's money. Perhaps she'd never decide and eventually pass it on to someone else, who'd dream of spending it on a trip to the moon, solar powered car or calorie free chocolate.

It wouldn't matter either way, as planning how to spend it would brighten many a rainy day and that's exactly what Great Aunt Dylis had intended it be used for.

2. Christmas Visitor

Mrs L. Wainwright, Flat 16c Camellia House

It's Christmas morning and I don't want to be alone. I won't be really alone, of course; other people live in the flats and my son, David, will telephone me. He's very good and calls me quite often. He put a lovely letter in with my card to tell me how well all the family are doing and how busy they are. There were pictures of the boys too; it's hard to believe that they're grown-up now. Maybe David, or one of the boys, will visit in the New Year, if they have time.

As I look around my home, I see it's not just my industrious family I should be thankful for. I have all the necessities of life; shelter, warmth and food. There are plenty of poor devils that won't see that this Yuletide, or any other day their whole lives, some of them. I have luxuries too; I treated myself to a good selection of tasty foods and I have beautiful gifts.

Christmas is about more than gifts and fancy food though. I think of it as a time for families, charity and traditional celebrations. David and his wife sent me some gift vouchers and a lovely big basket of toiletries. My daughter-in-law Patricia chose that, I expect, and had it gift wrapped in the shop to save a job in their busy lives. Some people say White Musk is rather old fashioned but I think it's quite nice really. It's almost as good as the floral scent I usually choose. Still, it's been a while since they've had time to visit me, I can't expect them to remember my tastes.

Shower gel, soap and body lotion are always useful. Shampoo and conditioners are perhaps less so. I always have my hair done at the hairdressers on the corner these days. I could do it myself, of course, but it gives me somewhere to go, people to talk to. Lovely girl that Sandra, always pleased to see me and I don't think it's just because of the small tip I give her.

I have a lovely lot of cards brightening up the flat. Reading the names and occasional snippets of news always helps me feel that people are close in thought, even though they're miles away. There's David and Patricia's huge one, one from Sandra and the other girls in the salon, two from old neighbours and one from the nice man who replaced my windows last month. There's even one from my youngest grandson. I think I like that best because he made it himself.

There aren't any decorations. I suppose I could have put up a few strands of tinsel, but that's not the kind of sparkle I want over the festive season.

Miss L. Wainwright, Flat 6c Camellia House

It's Christmas morning and I'm so glad I'm not on my own. Christmas is when family and friends get together to share gifts, good food and it's a great time for partying or a chance to spend time with just one special person, but never to be alone. I've got my wonderful baby daughter, Chloe. She loves me and I love her. I'll never turn my back on her the way my parents did to me, when they discovered she was expected.

We don't need anyone else and I don't mind that it's just us, or at least I've learnt to get used to it. We've got our health and a roof over our heads and enough to eat; that's more than some people can say. I've got the cutest present for little Chloe. She's at the age where she's going to be more interested in the wrapping than the gift, but I wanted to get her something. It's a pink fuzzy bobble hat, a real bargain from the charity shop. She made me a card. Of course, she didn't really know what she was doing, but the red and green scribbles look kind of festive and it shimmers with the glitter she sprinkled over it. I know my little angel would have made me a proper card if she could.

I'll put on the radio; that will be cheerful and make me feel in touch with the rest of the world.

Mrs L. Wainwright, Flat 16c Camellia House

What an awful racket! It must be that disgraceful girl with the beautiful baby. What the owner was thinking when he sold some of these flats to the council I shall never know! That single mother doesn't give the slightest thought to the convenience of anyone else. She's not exactly a friendly girl, although I suppose she's different with the boys. I know she's not married because sometimes the postman mixes up our mail. That reminds me, a card came for her yesterday. I really should have taken it down, but my feet were hurting and it isn't as though she won't have plenty of others. The card is propped up on the radiator cover right by the door ready for me to take it next time I go out.

She won't want an old lady like me bothering her today. I suppose she's having a party for all her friends. A young thing like that will have her family and plenty of people her own age popping in to see her and she's probably cooking a big meal. Not turkey, I don't suppose. Chinese food maybe, or something modern and interesting. Youngsters have no respect for tradition.

I thought of phoning David, but I don't suppose he'll want

to be bothered with me either and really he should be the one to call me.

Miss L. Wainwright, Flat 6c Camellia House

Crikey, what a racket! I'd hoped to listen to some proper carols or jokey festive songs. Still it does provide a bit of company, sort of. I'd better turn it down though, so I don't disturb anyone. The insulation between these flats doesn't work any better than the lift does. I daren't use it for fear of Chloe and I getting stuck again. Almost an hour it was last time before anyone heard my cries and got help.

I'm not sure who else is in the flats today. Most people have gone away. I expect the sour old baggage who lives above me will go out to have lunch with her friends. I think she's lived here a long time and old people always have a lot of friends, don't they? One of them sent her a card. I didn't realise it was for her until I'd got Chloe settled for the night and I couldn't leave her to take it up then. I'd go up now, but she won't want me interrupting her while she's getting ready to go out and I don't suppose she'll want Chloe near her at any time.

No one seems to want to bother with me now I have a child. I can't go clubbing with my old friends and I don't go anywhere to make new ones. There's no point in my trying to speak to my parents; I doubt they'll have changed their opinion of me. It's better they have no way of contacting me, then I won't be disappointed they don't try.

Mrs L. Wainwright, Flat 16c Camellia House

Lovely baby she's got – my namesake downstairs. To give the girl her due, she seems to care for the little girl reasonably well. The child is always clean and her mother wraps her up well before taking her out. It must be a struggle getting that pushchair up and down the stairs, but they go out every day. I see them in the park sometimes. I'd like to go and give the youngster some bread to throw for the ducks, or carry the child while she lugs the pushchair upstairs but it's not my place to interfere. How I long to hold a child again and feel that I'm important to someone.

Miss L. Wainwright, Flat 6c Camellia House

How adorable my sweet Chloe is. She doesn't like her though – my namesake upstairs. Probably thinks I'm a bad mother too, as she's always staring at Chloe as though expecting to see something wrong with her. She doesn't have a clue how difficult it is to cope with her all on my own; even when I'm struggling to get back into the flat, it's as much as Mrs Wainwright can do to hold the door open for me.

I shouldn't think like that. It's not her fault we've got nothing in common and it is Christmas. Maybe she's friendly once you get to know her and it's just me she doesn't like. Or the problem might be just that I've never bothered to get to know her. I should take up her card and wish her a Happy Christmas and let her see I'm not nearly as bad as she thinks I am.

Mrs L. Wainwright, Flat 16c Camellia House

I expect she's got a poor opinion of me; probably thinks I'm miserable and boring. She'd be right; it's Christmas day and I'm sat here on my own feeling sorry for myself.

Maybe it's partly my own fault? Although I wish my old friends would visit me, I never call on them. I have shown little interest in David and Patricia's life since they married and I've barely spoken to my neighbours. Would my situation improve if I behaved differently?

Miss L. Wainwright, Flat 6c Camellia House

What should I do with Chloe; get out the buggy or carry her? As soon as we leave the flat she's going to think we're going to the park. I might as well take her after I've delivered the card, we've nothing better to do and the turkey burgers will wait.

Mrs L. Wainwright, Flat 16c Camellia House

What shall I do with myself? Moping is no way to carry on. I'll pour myself a sherry and put the radio on.

Hmmm. That's the same music as I heard from downstairs. Maybe she's listening to the radio too? If so, she's on her own with the baby. I was sure she'd be having guests or going out as she's hardly bought any shopping the last few weeks. Oh! Perhaps she doesn't have much money? I've got more than enough food…

Miss L. Wainwright, Flat 6c Camellia House

Come on Chloe, you carry the card and I'll carry you. The sight of a child on Christmas morning just might be enough to break the ice.

Mrs L. Wainwright, Flat 16c Camellia House

I'll take down her card and invite her in for a drink and suggest we all eat together. After all, it is Christmas.

Miss L. Wainright, Flat 6c Camellia House

It's New Year's Eve; a time for fresh starts and hope. I've written a letter to my parents and enclosed a picture of Chloe. Maybe the sight of her beautiful smile will convince them she was worth losing a university place for, and allow me to forget their harsh words. I won't wait alone, waiting for a New Year to start and the mistakes of the past one to be forgotten.

Lorna Wainwright is coming down to visit me and Chloe. We got on so well when we shared Christmas lunch and took Chloe to feed the ducks that I know tonight will be fun. She told me how hadn't often seen her grandsons while they were growing up because of her disapproval of their mother and that she regrets being so stubborn. That's so sad as she loves children. I'm hoping that when Lorna gets to know us better she'll spend more time with Chloe. It will be such a relief to have someone to rely on.

Mrs L. Wainwright, Flat 16c Camellia House

It's New Year's Eve; a time for reflection and change.

I've realised that if I want my life to change I'll have to change myself too. I rang my son, rather than waiting to hear from him. When Patricia answered, I thanked her for my Christmas present and wished her a happy New Year before I asked to speak to David. He told me they were going to a party at a neighbour's home and that he hoped to come and see me in a few day's time. Instead of telling him how lonely I was, I assured him that I too was going out for the evening and said I would look forward to seeing him and Patricia whenever they were able to visit.

It's true; when they do visit, I'll have something positive to tell them, but until then I won't be alone. Tonight, I'm going down to visit Lucy and Chloe Wainwright. We got on so well when we shared Christmas lunch and took Chloe to feed the ducks that I'm sure this evening will be fun too.

I'm hoping that when Lucy gets to know me better, and learns she can trust me, she will allow me to care for Chloe sometimes. I know the sparkle in my eyes will be matched by that of the sweet little girl and her mother when they open the door to me this evening.

3. Surface Tension

The lake resembled a pool of mercury, gleaming in the sun. It created a perfect reflection of the cloudless blue sky. Not a breath of wind created the tiniest ripple. It was deceptive though, the water below must be teeming with life.

Mel stepped away from her husband, away from the words he was trying to form. She couldn't listen. She bent as close to the water as she could without risk of toppling in. An insect, a water-boatman, seemed to skate effortlessly, although in reality surely clinging on to his precarious existence. That was her and Pete. To those walking by, it looked as though they were OK. A happy couple out for a walk. The cynical perhaps might guess it was the calm before the storm. They'd be wrong though. For her the storm had already come. There would be no release for her – nor for Pete. She shouldn't think of it as her personal tragedy. It had been as tough for him. He'd wanted the baby as much as she had.

He had been strong. Reassuring when she started to bleed. Calm at the hospital, when they'd learned the baby, their child, no longer existed. He'd held her together when she crumbled and didn't let go until he knew she wouldn't fall apart. He'd soothed her as best he could, just as they might have soothed the child, had he lived.

When she was alone, Mel held herself tight and rocked. She made no sound, shed no tears. Like a baby she couldn't describe her pain, her loss. It was too much for words. Too much for tears or anger. For regret or blame. Just too much.

When she'd left a pack of condoms on his bedside table, Pete had understood. It wasn't an invitation to touch her. She hadn't been ready. Still wasn't.

Pete hadn't disintegrated until his mum said it was good it had happened early. Mel hadn't even started to show. People wouldn't know.

"We know," he'd said. "Mel and I had a baby. We couldn't see it, or feel it, but we loved it. Still do."

"You don't even know if it would have been a boy or a girl." His mum wasn't unsympathetic to their loss, she just didn't understand. "You can have another one, that should help."

Pete had understood though, how Mel felt. She thought she'd been alone in her grief. Thought they'd both been alone, side by side. It wasn't until he'd cried at his mother's words she'd realised how wrong she'd been.

He'd said they needed to talk. "Let's go for a walk."

They'd often done that, gone to neutral ground when there was something to discuss. It wasn't always bad. They'd walked for miles as they debated whether they could afford to buy a house and live together. Then walked miles further when Pete learned his company planned to relocate and the house, if she still wanted to share one with him, couldn't be in her beloved Pembrokeshire. Of course she'd gone with him. He hadn't really needed to ask. They'd never really needed to talk. Their long conversations had only served to show how much in agreement they were. They didn't talk to reach a compromise, to argue, to break bad news.

Mel shook her head. She wouldn't think of Pete breaking bad news now. There'd been enough of that. She'd do as she'd been doing for months now and pretend everything was OK. She'd act like that water-boatman skating over the surface. He looked fine. While the surface of the water stayed calm and ripple free he was safe. A splash, a storm or any kind of disruption and his world would be in turmoil, his brief life over. Like an unborn baby when his mother bled and carried him no more.

Him. How could she have said that, even to herself? Admit she'd named him in her heart for her father. The baby couldn't replace her lost father, yet she'd have loved him just as much. Another baby, people had told her, would be loved as much as the one she'd lost. Would help her. Maybe they weren't just empty words of comfort. Maybe they were the truth. Maybe.

What they couldn't tell her, what nobody knew, was whether the next one would live.

Pete wanted to talk, he'd said. She glanced at him. No, not wanted to, needed to. If she let him speak, he'd ripple the surface of their lives, she could see that. Perhaps that was what he needed to do.

Mel heard a child squeal. Saw him run towards her.

"Come back here," a woman's voice yelled. "Don't go near the water!"

Pete stiffened beside Mel, but it was all right. The boy stopped on the path. Waited.

A heavily pregnant woman approached."You mustn't run off like that," she scolded gently.

He hung his head. After a moment he looked up and smiled. "Bwead now?"

She took a slice from her bag and broke off a piece for him. "Be careful not to fall in," she warned.

Ducks must hear well or have an amazing sense of smell,

for soon six of them were paddling furiously towards the child. His mother repeatedly handed the boy small chunks of bread. The boy's aim wasn't good and he wobbled with each throw. His mother held tight to his sweater as he leaned toward the birds. They splashed and gobbled. He shrieked and threw. Soon the bread was gone and the waters muddied. The little family continued around the path. Their lunch guests swam away.

It would take a long time for the clarity of the water to return. The ripples soon disappeared though. The turbulence had brought the depths up into view, yet the surface was still calm. Maybe if she were to look, a water-boatman would come skating across the surface. Maybe the one she'd seen earlier had retreated from the chaos and disruption, only to emerge shaken but whole. She could look, but didn't need to. Such a thing must be possible, unlikely though it seemed. If not, there'd be no water-boatman after a storm.

Mel felt a gentle pressure on her hand. Pete was squeezing it, just as he had so often before when she'd needed comfort. Had he reached for her when the boy had gone too close to the lake, or had she reached for him? It didn't matter; they comforted each other. They'd needed to. They'd needed the silence too, or perhaps that was just Mel. Now though, perhaps it was time to see what lay below.

"John," she whispered. "I'd thought of calling him John."

"John's a good name. I like that."

Mel nodded. She couldn't say more. Couldn't look at him.

"Shall we do it then, call him John?" Pete said.

She said yes, or thought she did as she cried in his arms. There was plenty of time to think of a different name for their next child.

4. Life's An Adventure

"It had yellow spots on its head and all down the side of the shell, just like road markings," I said. I was snuggled up on the sofa with two of my grandkids and describing the yellow-spotted Amazon river turtle. "And it was about this big." I held my hands about three feet apart, and my elbows much wider. It was a something of an exaggeration but impressed my young listeners.

"Were there alligators?" my granddaughter Millie asked.

I hesitated for a moment. "No, love. They don't live in that part of the world."

I watched emotions play over the children's faces. There was disappointment that they wouldn't hear me describe wrestling alligators during my long ago trip kayaking the Amazon, but something else too.

They'd asked about piranhas just moments before and I'd reassured them I'd not been in danger of a shoal of them turning me into a skeleton in three seconds flat had I fallen in. Prior to that I'd admitted I never even caught a glimpse of the jaguars which are said to inhabit the banks of the mighty Amazon river. At the back of their minds, I'm sure, was the thought that if I wasn't making up those things to improve my story, just maybe I wasn't making up any of it.

"There weren't any alligators, but there was another animal with…" I used my arms to mime a huge set of jaws opening wide.

Both children leant forward a little.

I snapped the 'jaws' shut, right in front of their noses. They let out delighted squeals.

"Crocodiles!" Millie exclaimed.

"Dwarf caiman, actually," I said and described the fearsome looking creatures.

"But they're only small?" Millie asked.

"Small for a crocodile perhaps, but some were bigger than me."

"Really?" It was Jacob, the most sceptical of my grandchildren, who asked that.

"Oh yes, much bigger," I told him.

Well, I think they were at any rate. They'd certainly seemed massive when aged just eighteen, I'd seen them right up close. I moved on from the water creatures to not only describe, but demonstrate, the calls of howler monkeys and reenact the antics of tamarins and marmosets. Perhaps I did get a little carried away, especially when the children joined in, but it was good, harmless fun.

Once we'd all calmed down a bit, I sent Millie and Jacob up to get ready for bed. "I'll tell you the rest once you've brushed your teeth and put your pyjamas on," I promised.

I started the last instalment with a king vulture circling overhead, but as soon as I'd painted the dramatic scene, I reminded them it was way up high and that vultures are no threat to people. Then I told them of the beautiful birds, calling, flitting and swooping all around. They really were every colour of the rainbow and many of them almost too gorgeous to be true.

"One day, we paddled through a patch of cool shade under some rubber trees," I said. "Just as we came out into the sun again I saw a flash of the most incredible blue. I thought it might be a parrot, but it was there and gone in a second, so I couldn't be sure. Then it came back. I was right about it being a parrot; it was a hyacinth macaw. The bird landed on the front of my kayak and tilted its head to one side, showing off its wonderful blue plumage and the brilliant yellow around its eye."

"That's amazing, Nanna," Millie said sleepily. She kissed me goodnight and went up to bed.

"I'll be up to tuck you in, in just a minute," I promised, even though I was sure that by then she'd be asleep and dreaming of making a similar journey herself one day. She loves animals and has an adventurous spirit.

Once his little sister had left the room, sceptical Jacob asked, "Nanna, was this kayaking thing before or after the police chained you to the fence at Greenham Common?"

"Before. But it wasn't the police who chained us up, we did that ourselves."

"Why?"

I wanted to tell him a little of our fears over nuclear war, and encourage him to stand up for what he believed in, but also wanted him to get a good night's sleep, so decided that would have to wait. "Publicity," I said. "We did the same thing when they started building the bypass. You know that clump of big trees near the football field?"

"The ones Dad said wouldn't be there without you?"

"That's them." As I coaxed Jacob up to bed I described my pivotal role in saving that small patch of ancient woodland. I probably exaggerated a little. I often do; it's a family trait.

I remember my grandma telling me of the amazing places she'd been to with the synchronised swimming team she'd been part of, before the war.

"It was known as water ballet then," she'd said. "I like that name much better, but I'd love to have had the costumes and waterproof makeup the girls wear these days."

She told me she'd travelled on the Trans-Siberian railway, performed in a pool heated by lava flow and met royalty from a dozen different countries.

"You've had so many adventures!" I remember saying. I hadn't believed a word of it. I don't mean I thought she was a liar, it felt more as though she were making up tales as a change from reading to us about the *Famous Five* and *Secret Seven*.

"I have, love, but all of life is an adventure. You remember that."

I did remember, as she said it quite often. That wasn't the only way in which she repeated herself, but I always loved to listen. When she told me of the exciting things she'd done as a truck driver and mechanic during the war she was fond of pointing out her experiences were very similar to those experienced by the queen who was a fellow member of the Women's Auxiliary Territorial Service. I'd been thrilled, of course, but the idea of Queen Elizabeth and Grandma donning overalls and dashing about the country on vital war work was too fantastic to be entirely convincing.

Grandma told me that meeting my grandfather, getting married and having children was just as much of an adventure. She said the same about her first post war job, setting up home, and becoming a grandparent. I found those stories interesting too, but as they were less exciting I preferred to hear about her military and swimming exploits.

"Did you win any competitions?" I'd asked.

"Oh yes, heaps. We were given rosettes, silver cups and

crystal vases almost every week," Grandma declared proudly.

"What about an olympic medal?" I'd asked, eagerly.

She'd hesitated for a moment. "No, sadly not. Synchronised swimming has only become an Olympic sport quite recently."

That made we wonder if there was more truth in her stories than I'd previously thought possible. It would have been easy, and fun, for her to tell me she'd won gold. I was sure she'd been tempted to do just that, but resisted.

Grandma had swum with us when we were little, I seemed to remember, and she still drove her small car well into her nineties, but that and a handful of newspaper clippings were the nearest we children had to any proof she'd really done all she claimed. There were few pictures in the old newspapers, none of them clear and the reports about Mary Jones were so dull compared to Grandma's version that I paid them little attention. By the time Grandma embarked on her final 'adventure' of moving into a retirement home, I seriously doubted any of her stories had been based on facts. I did however admire the optimistic way she looked forward to making new friends in the home, and to having all the cooking and cleaning done for her so she could put her remaining energy into having fun.

When Grandma died her estate was divided up amongst her nine grandchildren. We each got a few thousand pounds and a letter expressing her wish that we use the money to enjoy an adventure, and the hope we'd share the memories with our own grandchildren one day. She also reminded us that although some parts might seem more exciting than others, all of life was an adventure.

The handwritten and individually addressed letters were almost identical. The money was shared absolutely equally. They would have been enough, I'm sure, to convince each of us to carry out her wishes, but we were also given a unique item, just for ourselves. I don't recall them all, but one cousin, an engineer, received something small and metallic which meant nothing to me, but made his eyes open wide.

"It was all true," he'd whispered, making me guess it was something connected with her war work.

My own heirloom was a small piece of plastic; a nose clip, just like those used by synchronised swimmers. Its cracked and brittle appearance told me it was old and I suddenly had no doubt that Grandma had worn it whilst performing water ballet routines with her team. Perhaps sometimes they really had swum in pools heated by lava flow or before the crowned heads of Europe.

You've maybe guessed I spent my legacy on a trip kayaking on the Amazon and you know I've shared my memories with my grandchildren. I'm not sure they believe half of it. To tell the truth I do sometimes wonder myself which are genuine memories and which have been embroidered by my recent internet research. Exaggeration is a family trait, but so is treating life as an adventure.

Starting university would have been daunting had it not been for the confidence gained on my travels up the Amazon the summer beforehand, and my determination to consider my education as an adventure. I've tackled all life's big moments that way, from marrying Chaz to setting up home and then a business together. Bringing my own children into the world, and seeing them do the same might seem ordinary by some standards, but that too has been a wonderful adventure. My life hasn't been constant joy, but there have been far more good times than bad and I think that's partly thanks to the adventurous frame of mind passed on to me by my grandmother.

One day my own grandchildren will receive a letter from me declaring my hope that their share of my estate helps them to enjoy an adventure and that eventually they'll share the memories with their grandchildren. I'll also remind them that life is the biggest adventure of all.

They'll each receive a small memento too. Jacob's will be a rusted padlock, cut open with bolt cutters. Millie's will be a vibrantly coloured feather. I'd like it to be a gorgeous blue wing feather dropped by a hyacinth macaw. That may not be possible, because although it's true that I once got an incredibly close view of one of those beautiful and extremely rare birds, it didn't shed a feather. I have a feeling they're now protected to the extent that collecting a feather is probably illegal as well as unlikely. There are other colourful birds in the Amazon though. Looking up the details of the turtles, caimans and agile tamarins not only refreshed my memory enough to tell good stories, it made me want to return. Why not? I'm only sixty-three. I have a lot more life to live and there are many more adventures to be had.

5. If A Thing's Worth Doing

Act 1

"Dad, I'm going to be on telly, just like you!" Tim yelled. He jumped into the car.

Daniel sighed. Because Tim had learning difficulties, he didn't always understand things easily, but Daniel had tried to explain and he'd been sure Tim had understood. "No, Tim. We talked about this, remember? You're not going to be in the school play."

"I am, Dad. Miss Davies said I could and she said I'd be on the telly and make you proud of me."

Daniel gritted his teeth. "Miss Davies is wrong, Tim. You aren't going to be in the play and it won't be on the telly."

She was wrong about Daniel being proud of his son too, but he wouldn't tell Tim that. Poor lad had enough problems in his life. His mother left when he was a baby, he struggled with schoolwork, with co-ordination, with everything really. Tim had all his father's love of performing, but little of his talent. Daniel loved his boy, admired his cheerfulness in the face of hurdles and setbacks, but how could he ever be proud of Tim's performance in a school play? Daniel had very nearly been nominated for a BAFTA. Tim would barely be able to read a few lines, let alone remember and perform them. It wasn't fair to expect him to try. If a thing wasn't done well, then it wasn't worth doing; that was Daniel's motto.

"But Miss Davies said…"

"I'll talk to Miss Davies. Now, what would you like for tea?"

"Pizza!"

"OK."

"Yay!"

If there was anything Tim could do well, then it was to eat pizza. He'd have it every day if he could – which was just as well because Daniel couldn't cook.

Act 2

Daniel tried to make Miss Davies understand why Tim couldn't be in the play.

"But he will do it well," the teacher said. "He's so excited by this and has been telling all his friends how you'll help him, so he'll be really good and how he'll be on the telly…"

"What is this about being on TV?" If Daniel played it right he might at least wangle an interview to plug his latest film. Almost nothing was more important than publicity.

"It was explained in the letter we sent all parents about the play."

Daniel hadn't read it. Because Tim wasn't to appear in the play, a letter on the subject was of no interest.

"As you know, the play is an attempt to raise much needed funds," Miss Davies said. "The local TV station are going to do a piece at the dress rehearsal. That should help us sell more tickets and I admit that having your son in the cast would be an added draw, but that's not the real reason I'm hoping you'll allow Tim to take part."

"So, what is?" Presumably it wasn't just an attempt to humiliate him, but he could easily imagine the headlines when Tim appeared as the back end of a horse or fluffed his lines.

"Tim said if he was good enough to be on telly like you, then you'd be pleased. Mr Berkeley, he idolises you and wants to please you. If he could feel he'd done that it would be so good for his confidence."

Daniel swallowed. He'd told himself he'd wanted to spare Tim from humiliation, but it wasn't true. Daniel hadn't been thinking of his son's wishes and certainly hadn't considered helping the school that had done so much for Tim.

"I'll talk to Tim," Daniel said without committing himself to anything.

Act 3

"Miss Davies said to tell you why I want to be in the play."

"Why do you, Tim?"

"I was going to be a sheep. Sheep are nice and Niall was going to be a sheep as well. We've been practising baa-ing." Tim demonstrated with a great deal of enthusiasm. Daniel had to admit he did sound rather like an excited sheep.

"Niall was going to be a sheep too?" Why would Tim's friend agree to such a lowly role? He was a bright kid, surely capable of learning a more demanding part.

"Yes. He's lots better than me at maths and writing but not so good at baa-ing as me. I'm the best." He again demonstrated his proficiency at sheep imitations.

With anyone else, his agent or a director for example, Daniel would have thought he was being manipulated, but Tim wasn't like that. Tim was his biggest fan and kindest critic. He'd never be a professional actor and probably not a professional anything, but he was a good kid who did his best at everything he tried.

Daniel was the one in the wrong. He's not been a very good dad, but he's the best Tim has. If he can't see that Tim's opinion is worth more than anything that producers and directors could say, he's a worse dad and more shallow person than he realised. It was worthwhile being Tim's father and from now on he was determined he'd try his best to be good at that task.

Act 4

Daniel came into school with Tim before the dress rehearsal and showed the cast the breathing exercises he used to help his nerves before important performances. He was glad of the opportunity to use them himself.

He needn't have worried, the rehearsal went well and when the sheep came onto the stage they were completely covered in wool. Daniel had no trouble identifying his son though, as he really was by far the best at baa-ing.

"That's Tim. That's my son," he told everyone who'd listen, including the television reporter.

"You must be very proud of him," she said.

"Yes, yes I am. Tim worked hard to gain and perform this role. If a thing's worth doing it's worth doing to the best of your ability, that's my motto."

"Can we use that on the report and then perhaps you'd like to tell us about your latest movie?"

"By all means quote me as saying how proud I am of my son, but I can't stay for an interview. I have a more important appointment – I'm taking Tim and his friends out for a pizza."

Curtain

6. None So Blind

Norma didn't know what to do, so as usual she did nothing and ignored what was happening almost under her nose.

"No, Jamie. I said you can't have them." A woman snatched the crisps from her son's grasp and shoved them back on the shelf. Anger crackled from her like a static charge.

Norma kept her distance, but it was too late. The shock had jolted her out of the supermarket and sent her tumbling into the past. A child cried, either Norma's seven-year-old sister from sixty years ago or the toddler strapped securely into the trolley just feet away. Norma couldn't tell but it didn't matter. The child should be quiet. If they'd just be quiet everything would be OK.

The cries subsided, replaced by a mischievous giggle. Not Jean then. Norma's sister had never giggled after she'd stopped crying. Norma allowed her mind to focus again on the present. That was a mistake. She saw the boy drop another huge pack of crisps into the trolley. Norma walked faster, keeping her head turned away. With luck she'd be at the end of the aisle and out of sight before anything happened.

As she drew level she heard the mother say 'no'. Well, not say it; yell it. Clearly she was losing patience; had lost it. The mother took the crisps and hurled them back on the shelf.

The boy screamed, "Want it, want it!" He lurched in his

seat to snatch at another bag.

The mother raised a hand.

Norma willed her legs to move her away or her eyes to close so she wouldn't have to see the slap. Neither happened. This time she'd have to witness the violence. Have to acknowledge it. Would have to do something.

Norma tasted acid in her throat. There was a metallic clatter. The boy screamed. His mother's hand crashed down on the edge of the trolley, not his fragile face.

"I didn't hit him," the mother whispered. It didn't seem she was speaking to Norma, more that she was reassuring herself.

"Jamie, you're making Mummy angry. You can't have any more crisps. I've already told you."

"Want it, want it."

The mother manoeuvred the trolley into the centre of the aisle so he couldn't reach the tempting packages. She almost pushed a wheel over Norma's foot.

"Sorry," she muttered without looking up.

She hadn't even noticed Norma.

The woman spoke gently to the boy, explaining crisps weren't healthy and she'd buy him some nice bananas instead. Although too young to understand her logic the soothing words calmed him.

'Nabanana, want nabanana," he said cheerfully.

Norma's breathing and heart rate returned to normal. The boy would be OK. His mother would probably lose her temper again but she'd do nothing worse than shout out her frustration. Norma didn't need to do anything to protect him. This wasn't the same as the beatings her big sister had endured. The beatings Norma had only fully understood last week when her father had been buried. Jean attended the funeral, but only after Norma had begged her.

"All right, I'll come for you, not for him," Jean had said.

"Why are you still like that? I know I was his favourite when we were kids, but you can't still be jealous about that, can you?"

Jean didn't reply.

"Never went back to see him once did you? Just left at eighteen and didn't come back. Why?" Norma asked.

"Couldn't go before, could I? Had to wait until you were old enough to get away yourself, if you'd needed to."

It was then Norma learned her sister's childhood bruises weren't the result of clumsiness. Norma was the happy, confident one. She did well at school and fussed over her father, warming his slippers and stirring his tea. Jean was sullen and quiet. She never raised her hand in class and didn't lift a finger to help her father unless she had to. No wonder Daddy loved Norma and didn't like Jean.

After the funeral, Norma's grief for the father was mixed with the guilt she felt over having been blind to Jean's suffering. She should have noticed, should have done something. At the start she'd been no older than the boy who'd thrown a tantrum when he couldn't have crisps; too young to understand what was happening. She'd got older though. Would have seen what was happening if she'd looked, if she'd been prepared to risk losing her favoured position and be beaten herself. Somehow she'd blocked it all out.

Because she couldn't admit to herself that her father was hitting her sister, she couldn't blame him. Instead she'd blamed Jean for being cold towards him, for upsetting and abandoning him once she turned eighteen. Resented Jean for refusing to visit, and making her feel guilty for lying to their father and sneaking out to see her.

Norma was still blaming Jean. She'd hated her for revealing the man she'd adored wasn't the loving father she'd managed to convince herself he was. He'd never raised a hand against Norma, but still hurt her emotionally by spoiling her relationship with Jean. Norma was still acting as his weapon. When confronted by the truth, she'd accused Jean of lying and refused to say another word to her.

Norma abandoned her shopping trolley and left the store. She was ringing Jean's doorbell less than twenty minutes later.

"Can you come with me, Jean? Right now?" she asked as soon as the door was opened.

"I could, but I'm not sure I want to."

"Please. I knew you were telling me the truth about Dad. I suppose I'd always known really." She hung her head, unable to meet Jean's gaze.

"Don't blame yourself, Norm. If you'd tried to stop him he'd just have belted you as well and I wouldn't have wanted that." Jean reached out and squeezed her sister's shoulder. "So, where is it you want to take me?"

"The cemetery."

"Don't ask me to forgive him, Norm. I can't do it."

"That's not why we're going. Come on."

Norma led the way to her father's graveside. "Daddy, you shouldn't have hit Jean, she didn't deserve it. I should have stopped you. It's too late for that, but I can stop you hurting either of us again."

It wasn't nearly enough, but at last she had done something.

7. The Truth About Charlotte

"I'm a complete idiot," I wailed into the phone.

"True." Seventy-three years wasn't long enough to teach my brother tact.

"Thanks a lot!"

"You know me, never argue with a lady," Phil said.

"So you admit I'm a lady?"

"A direct descendent of the Great Charlotte Yonge surely must be."

"Don't, oh please don't."

"Oh, Sis, what've you discovered now? Seven illegitimate children? She plagiarised everything? Took money out the church collection?"

"Don't be silly."

"You're the idiot, remember. I know – rum smuggling!"

"You're not helping." He was though. There was nothing he could do, but at least I could tell him my troubles.

"Shall I come round, Charlie?" he offered as soon as I tried to start.

It didn't take him long to reach me – we've stayed close in more than one way. Phil hugged me tight then demanded tea and cake. "I can't be sympathetic on an empty stomach."

"True, nor on a full one," I teased. Just having my brother there had cheered me a little.

"I can try."

I knew he would. Once he had his tea, and a generous wedge of my lemon drizzle cake, I explained. "Great Granddad was born Nathaniel Robert Price."

"Not Yonge?"

"No."

"Ah." To be fair, I think my brother did try not to smirk.

"Miss Yonge was his godmother. At her request he took her name."

"So we're kind of adopted descendants? That makes a lot of sense."

"How does it?" I asked.

"Well, I'd wondered how a deeply religious, Victorian spinster managed to have direct ancestors."

Obviously I should have wondered that myself. Instead I'd jumped straight to the conclusion I'd wanted. My foster daughter Saffy started me off. Ego surfing it's called, apparently; when you look yourself up on the internet. I typed in my name and got hits for the woman who became my obsession. One Charlotte Mary Yonge was a marvel, the other, me, has done nothing with my life.

She, the marvel, started teaching aged seven and continued for more years than I've been alive. She wrote forty novels, plus poems, plays and stories, edited a magazine, even named a village. All that in the days before women could vote.

I didn't tell Phil any of that. He knew. Everyone I've met in the last few years knows all about Charlotte. My obsession you see. I've been writing articles for magazines, newspapers and the internet telling people of her many virtues. That was hard enough with a computer to research, check the spelling and send documents for me. She must have scratched out her words with something not much better than a quill and worked by candlelight.

Now many of her books are available again. There's a bronze statue of her and she has a web page. Nicest of all, I think, are the paving stones engraved with her words. I can't take much credit for these ideas, but like to think my efforts to have Charlotte properly recognised helped initiate them.

Phil squeezed my hand. "Sorry, Sis. I thought it was a kind of joke, us being related to her. I mean Yonge isn't exactly a common name, but …"

"But it's obvious to anyone but me that I'm not her great-great-granddaughter and I wasn't named after her. Of course I wasn't. You did try to tell me, didn't you?"

"I admit I wasn't as sure about the relationship as you."

That almost made me cry. Phil usually likes to say 'told you so' but then, when he was more entitled than ever to do so, he refrained.

"Does it really matter? We carry her name and our ancestor was a godchild. That kind of relationship would have been important to her."

"Yes, but… oh see for yourself." I shoved the papers towards him.

Phil looked through them. "No, I'm afraid there's no chance we're blood relatives."

"Of who?"

"This Mary Charlotte… oh."

"Yeah. Not only are we not related, it's not even her." The birth certificate I'd been sent was for someone else, born in a different place and a different time to Charlotte Mary Yonge.

Phil laughed. Actually laughed. "Oh dear, Sis. You

properly got it wrong, didn't you?"

"Thanks a lot!" I said. Again.

"You ninny. You learnt about an extraordinary woman and helped get her recognised. Does it really matter that you're not related?"

"It will tomorrow when I'm called to unveil that statue and have to admit I'm a fraud."

"But you're not. Look." He tapped the advert for the big opening. In it I'm described as 'namesake' not 'relative'. Phil had suggested I not claim a relationship until I could prove it. The papers I'd got that morning where supposed to be the proof.

"So you're the only one who'll know how stupid I've been?"

"I'm your big brother, it's not breaking news to me."

"Thanks a lot!" I said yet again. That time I meant it.

"What's really bugging you?" he, ever the perceptive one, asked.

"I just feel… like a nobody. She did so much and…"

"You've done nothing. Well, you did save me from drowning, selfish of me but I don't think that's nothing."

True, I pulled him out the canal, but that was an instinctive reaction which took what, twenty minutes of my life?

"And those cartoons you draw make people laugh. Laughter's important."

Maybe, but it's not a proper job like a teacher, writer or editor.

"How are your foster kids?" he changed the subject. Tactful at last?

"Paul wrote yesterday wishing me luck for the unveiling. He can't go but Oliver and Simon have promised to send photos. They're going and of course Lynne and Saffy will be there. Laura is about to be a grandmother again. Sonia's daughter has been accepted for Portsmouth Uni and says she'd like to visit some weekends… "

Phil interrupted. "How many of those kids you rescued from abuse or neglect will you be looking in the eye tomorrow and saying you're a nobody with nothing to show for your life?"

My tears dripped onto the table. "Oh, Phil. I've been a complete idiot."

"Told you so."

8. A Different Kind Of Enemy

My name is Matthew King; no one calls me that though. My parent's called me Mattie right from the start. That's what my wife, God rest her, called me too. The lads, when I joined up, called me 'Super' on account of the super king sized cigarettes I'd smoke whenever I got hold of them. Usually it was just roll ups, but you know the military, never let the truth get in the way of a good story.

Most often these days I'm called Gramps. That suits me just fine; I'm pleased that my daughter's boy spends so much time with me. I don't like it so much when my daughter uses the nickname too, cheeky girl that one. I love her though and young Jack, that's why I eventually took notice of what she had to say.

It's the smoking see, she never liked it, Julie didn't. Was often on at me to quit. I didn't take much notice. I thought it was just her cheeking me again. I was still serving in the Regiment when she started on at me. Heard it was bad for your health she had. Of course, I didn't believe it then, plenty of my army buddies smoked and there was nothing wrong with them.

There were three of us used to hang about together quite a lot. Roadrunner who never touched a fag and ran marathons, myself and Red. Red smoked a lot even by my standards and was a pretty good boxer. We all reckoned he could have turned professional, but he wanted to serve his country. Got more medals than me and Roadrunner put together and I like to think we didn't disgrace ourselves. There was that time… sorry; military battles aren't what this story's about. This time I'm fighting a much trickier enemy.

I'd lost touch with Red until his wife tracked me down. The guy was in hospital, would I go visit him? I'd heard that, when he retired from the military, he'd become a boxing coach. I'd expected him to have a broken jaw after pushing the next Joe Calzaghe a bit too far. I was wrong.

Red was slowly dying from some problem with his lungs. Been in a bad way for a couple of years I learnt. Chronic obstructive pulmonary disease is what he had. Red had on an oxygen mask and it took me a while to understand his wheezy way of talking. He wasn't strong enough to open a packet and strike a match even if they'd let him, but the cigarettes were still killing him.

I asked the doctor what could be done.

"Nothing for him now I'm afraid, except to keep him as comfortable as possible."

"You mean once anyone's got this thing, it's game over?"

"The lung damage is permanent, but if a smoker gives up then the condition can be improved. Your friend didn't stop, so his condition continued to worsen."

Right, I thought, I don't want a slow lingering death, I'm quitting.

Thinking and doing aren't the same though, are they? I'd smoked for more than fifty years. That's a mighty big habit to break. I did try, but found myself sitting in front of the telly, a lit fag in my hand, without realising what I'd done.

You'll realise seeing Red like that upset me, I didn't let that stop me visiting him though. I felt guilty in a way. Quite a few of the fags he'd smoked had been mine. I didn't know, not then, how dangerous they were. Well, I kidded myself, but there were warnings, even my little girl knew the truth.

Anyway, I had some good news after that. It was young Jack. Just fourteen and he'd tried to join the Regiment. Of course, they didn't let him. They gave him leaflets and one of those new fangled DVD things though, so he could start to prepare.

"I'm going to do everything they said, Gramps," he told me. "I want to be a hero, just like you."

Well I don't know about hero, but I certainly felt damn good to hear he was proud of me.

"I'm going to get really fit and I'm going to learn all about the unit's history, in case they ask about that on the interview."

"I'll help you, Jack," I promised.

I could help with training, as for the history, well crikey, hadn't I made some of it? It wasn't that easy though. I showed the lad a couple of press ups and I was coughing so much I couldn't tell him what to do. I timed his laps running round the park, but had to sit on a bench 'cause I was wheezing so much from the walk over there.

Then Julie called me. "I'm worried about Jack."

Well, that got my attention right away.

"He's started smoking."

I think I've said I didn't take much notice when she said she wanted me to stop, but this was different. She was right to be worried about her boy and when I thought of Red I knew she was right to worry about the ciggies too.

She told me she'd had a row with the lad about his smoking, so I suggested he come to me for a bit; see if he'd listen to me. Whilst he was there, I made a real effort to cut back. Couldn't really tell him not to do it though, not when I did myself.

I took him to see Red. That did it. The lad was worried about me I could tell. That's when it hit me. Jack and I could give up together, as a team. We'd stand a better chance and I'd really be doing something to help him. We knew it was going to be a hard fight and decided we shouldn't wait until we were in trouble before calling for reinforcements.

Julie hugged both of us when we said we were quitting. "That's fantastic news,"

"We have to work out a plan of campaign," I said.

First, we got to know the enemy. We read a lot of stuff on the internet. Nicotine is the stuff that gets you hooked, it stimulates the brain and giving up creates withdrawal symptoms. I knew I'd be getting problems that way, my body was used to a considerable daily dose. There's other bad stuff in cigarette smoke; at least fifty different harmful chemicals which can lead to a whole bunch of diseases and not just in the lungs either. I didn't like to think of all that pumping round young Jack's body.

Of course, non smokers can get sick too, but why increase the risk? That'd be like loading the enemy's guns for them! We got weapons of our own. Gum and patches were my first lines of defence and the lad and I signed up with an anti smoking support group. There we were advised on ways to get out the habit.

"Tell everyone you've stopped, so they don't offer you cigarettes. Hopefully they'll remind you, if you're tempted to smoke."

I knew Roadrunner would. Julie too of course. She had another suggestion.

"Remove temptation, Dad. Get rid of any cigarettes you've got left and all your ashtrays and lighters. You won't be able to smoke at home then, not without a bit of effort."

"Good idea, I found it's easy to light up without thinking. I'll ask around, see if anyone wants my lighters."

"If you know anyone you want to get cancer then give them your lighters and encourage them to carry on."

"Hey!" I was just about to say that wasn't fair, then I remembered how I felt about the fags I'd given Red.

"I'll see if the museum are interested in the oldest ones and chuck out the rest."

Jack put his lighter in the bin. I did the same with the one in my pocket and the almost full packet of cigarettes. Then we went round my house and found every lighter and ashtray. Julie was determined that I had no excuse for giving up on the giving up.

All this was a couple of weeks ago. I've not smoked, but I use the patches regular and chew the gum. Jack didn't need anything like that, lucky for him he hadn't got addicted. I reckon he'll do well in the military. He doesn't follow everyone else, he leads by example. He took some info on the diseases you can get from smoking to show his mates.

"None of them are cool," he told 'em and I think they must have agreed, 'cause he says that they never smoke around him now. Perhaps some of them have given up too. Hope so.

I've got a new nickname now. Instead of 'Super' for the superkings, Roadrunner started calling me 'Nosmo.' You gotta feel sorry for anyone who asks what it means.

"No Smo-King," I explain and then I give them the full story.

9. Sisters At The Seaside

Gladys had been looking forward to the seaside coach trip for months. It wasn't that she didn't go out much – she was fortunate in that kind friends and relatives often took her for a drive, a meal, or to some entertainment or other. She enjoyed them all, but the coach trip was different – just the idea of it reminded her of some of the best days of her youth. Of course it wouldn't be quite like it was when she'd done the same thing as a child. She'd known that from the start. Now, thanks to a certain person, it wouldn't be anything like the same. Even so, Gladys would not let anything, or anyone, spoil her day.

She tied on her headscarf and checked her reflection in the mirror. Good, all nice and tidy. Her nice coat was probably far thicker than she needed at this time of year, but sea breezes could be chilly and it looked smart. Her bag was packed ready with everything she might need and she was in plenty of time. Too early really, she thought as she set off.

The charabanc, as she liked to think of the coach, wouldn't reach the post office for nearly half an hour and it would take no more than ten minutes to walk there. Gladys needed to be early though, to ensure she found a seat nowhere near Betty.

Bournemouth they were going to. Gladys hadn't been there since she was a little girl. Back then a trip to the seaside was a once a year luxury, laid on by Dad's works.

How everyone had loved it! Mum handing out barley sugar with her hands dry for a change instead of doing the washing up, scrubbing their clothes or peeling potatoes. Dad teaching them to swim, then pretending to fall asleep so she and Betty could bury him in the sand.

The sisters used to share an ice cream, taking a lick each in turn. That way they could have another one to look forward to before they went home. They'd spend hours peering into rock pools, then searched the beach for shells and pretty stones. Betty had loved the tiny white shells curled just like miniature cream horns and Gladys had given her any she spotted. In return Betty had looked out for the stones with holes through which fascinated Gladys. She still had an especially pretty one her sister had found and threaded onto ribbon for her one birthday. Of course she never wore it now!

Odd, the street seemed deserted. Early as it was, she'd expected a few people to be making their way towards the post office. When she'd tentatively suggested the outing, as part of the village's bicentenary celebrations, she'd not been sure it would even be considered, especially not with Betty on the committee. Someone must have over-ruled her though, or maybe she'd been unaware who'd suggested it, as the idea was unanimously accepted and the trip quickly arranged.

Every ticket had sold out within a week of them being offered. Gladys took hers from her pocket and checked it again. She definitely had the right day and time. No location was printed onto her ticket, but the vicar himself had suggested she board at the post office.

"The coach can only make a few stops, if we're to get away on good time. One will be the church, the second the crossroads, and finally the post office. I think that will be best for you?"

"It would, yes," Gladys had agreed.

To take that route the coach would need to pass right by the end of her lane, where she caught the bus into town. It was probably Betty's idea to leave that one out. Gladys wouldn't say anything though. Unlike some people she wasn't petty and it did make sense to have just a few pick up points. They'd done that back when she was a child. Meeting friends and seeing everyone in their best clothes at the stop had been the start of the fun. Besides, she could manage that walk easily and would have plenty of time to rest on the journey there and back.

Why then could she see only one other person, making her way towards the post office from the opposite direction?

Oh no, not her! The woman was a long way off and well wrapped up against a possible unseasonal change in the weather, but Gladys would know that walk anywhere. Gladys had realised she'd have to put up with being on the same coach as her sister, but had expected Betty's irritating presence to be diluted by plenty of friends and neighbours.

They hadn't spoken for four months and Betty needn't think that would change just because they were the only two at the bus stop for a few minutes. Gladys slowed her pace. Why was Betty even joining the charabanc from this stop? The cross roads would have been closer for her. Not much admittedly. They used to go to the tea shop opposite the post office every Tuesday and reckoned it was the halfway point between their two homes.

"Neutral territory," Betty had joked back then when they hadn't been at war.

It was so stupid that they were now. A tiny disagreement,

over what Gladys couldn't quite recall, had somehow got out of hand. Even so, if Betty were to say she was sorry, Gladys would accept her apology.

"Or you could say sorry to her," Gladys' daughter had suggested.

"I will not. She started it, she should end it. Stubborn, that's her trouble." She'd decided to ignore the reply about pots and kettles.

They'd squabbled sometimes as children, Gladys and Betty. They'd been so alike they'd always wanted the same thing. They squabbled over the dresses and skirts cousin Milly passed on to them, they both wanted Mum to plait their hair first or to be the one to help ice the cake for Sunday tea. Those arguments had never lasted long though. If they couldn't agree, Mum would say no one would do it. If they didn't share, Dad would say he'd take away whatever they were battling over. That soon had them seeing sense!

When it came to things neither of them wanted, such as the job of hanging out the washing or fetching in the coal they did it together to get it over with quickly. Although it wasn't on purpose, they'd had the measles together too. That hadn't made their quarantine period any shorter, but at least they'd had company when they were forced to stay indoors all day, every day.

A cold, that was it! Betty claimed Gladys had given her a cold and said she shouldn't have met her that week if she was infectious. Really though she was covering up for the fact she'd had it first and passed it on to Gladys. Selfish, that's what it was, especially as Gladys had a new grandchild she'd had to avoid for a few days. Betty maintained she'd not even had a ticklish throat that Tuesday and Gladys had infected her, which had made her miss an important bowls match.

"A silly game! How can that be important?" Gladys had asked.

"I've been practising for months and we had a good chance, but because of you I let my whole team down," Betty claimed.

"Well, I missed seeing little Sophie's first smile."

"It's only wind at that age, you know it is."

Maybe Gladys' remark about Betty knowing more about wind than smiles had been just the tiniest bit unkind, but there had been no call for Betty to react quite so badly.

"Feeling rotten after your colds just made you both grumpy," Gladys' daughter said.

There was probably some truth in that, Gladys admitted to herself.

Drag her steps as she might, Gladys still arrived at the post office with plenty of time to spare. Betty, although moving at snail's pace herself, arrived soon after. They both checked their watches. Each of them took out their ticket, read it again, folded it in half and returned it to their pocket so it was ready to show the driver.

Gladys had to force herself not to chuckle as they mirrored each others actions while trying to seem as though neither had noticed the other. She couldn't help remembering the times they'd each made Mum very similar cards, regularly donated the same thing to the church raffle or turned up at events dressed almost identically. The last time that happened they'd had people in stitches by each putting on lipstick as though their sister were their reflection in a mirror.

As a giggle threatened to escape, Gladys covered it by

snapping, "Why are you here anyway? You should have got picked up at the cross roads."

"I couldn't. The charabanc is only making a few stops and the committee decided one should be by your lane instead of at the cross roads. With you being older, that seemed fair."

Cheek! Gladys wasn't even eighteen months older than Betty and, except when she was given her sister's cold, was perfectly fit. Besides Betty was wrong, wasn't she? The coach was stopping at the crossroads. Gladys pointed that out.

"No, Gladys," Betty replied. "Obviously you weren't paying attention as usual. The vicar definitely said it would stop at the lane and not the cross roads."

"No he didn't… " Gladys was going to suggest that just for once Betty accepted that she was in the wrong when a car pulled up.

The vicar wound down his window. "Would you ladies like a lift to the coach stop?"

"This is where you told us to wait," Betty told him.

"No, surely not? I must have got myself in a muddle. I'd arranged for it to stop at the cross roads and the end of the lane so neither of you had too walk to far. After passing on my cold to you both, it seemed the least I could do."

Betty and Gladys both looked at each other, raised their eyebrows and then shrugged. It was true that he'd had a cold around the same time as they had, though Gladys couldn't remember if he'd had it first or not. She guessed Betty would be equally unsure. As for the vicar getting in a muddle, well she had her ideas about that. It was because of his suggestions that so often both sisters made a lemon drizzle cake as a raffle prize, but then that was his favourite sweet treat and he did buy a lot of tickets.

"You're both always so punctual that when the coach arrived before you, I thought I'd best come looking for you."

Betty glanced at her watch. "Heavens! It's almost ten past!"

Together Gladys and Betty reached for the front door handle of the vicar's car. Then they both stopped and reached for the back one. There simply wasn't time to argue about it, so they scrambled in the back together. By the time they boarded the coach there were just three empty seats. One was at the front, next to the vicar's wife, so naturally they left that for him and took the two together further down.

They settled themselves in, then each took out a pink and white striped paper bag. Both hesitated, then without a word, offered their bags to each other. Gladys took a piece of barley sugar from Betty's bag, as Betty took an identical sweet from her sister's.

They didn't speak for a few minutes, as they were too busy laughing. When they did, every conversation began, "Do you remember the time we ...?"

Of course the answer was always 'yes' as so many of their happiest memories where shared ones. They'd make many more, and if the vicar were rash enough to fall asleep on the beach, they might well start by burying him in the sand. Not too deep though. He was a nice man and besides, they'd want to keep their energy for rock pooling, collecting shells and pebbles and queuing for ice creams.

10. Stepping On The Cracks

Tracey placed her feet carefully as she forced herself to walk towards the hospital. If she didn't step on the cracks maybe everything would be OK? She almost smiled as she saw how silly it was for a grown woman to be thinking like that. It had never worked before and wouldn't work now. Dad had insisted she visit yesterday. She hadn't and that disobedience would be unforgivable.

Unforgivable to him that was. Tracey was able to forgive herself. She'd actually been in a taxi on the way to the hospital when the nurse rang and apologetically passed on Dad's command. It hadn't been him she was on the way to see though. She'd had a call saying a donor organ was available for one of her patients and was being couriered over. Tracey just had time to get scrubbed up before it would arrive.

She'd refused to delay her arrival by visiting Dad. The anger he'd feel wouldn't be good for his heart, but any delay in the operation could mean death for the little girl who was being prepped to receive a new one. Besides, a row with Dad wouldn't leave her in a suitable frame of mind for the delicate surgery.

"Tell him I can't come now, but I'll visit tomorrow at ten." One of the perks of being a doctor in the hospital was that the usual visiting hours could be sidestepped.

The operation went well. There was every chance the little girl would go on to have a long and happy life. This child at least had the support of two loving parents and that would help.

Afterwards Tracey had nearly stopped to see her own father but she was too drained to cope with him. It wouldn't help anyway. Nothing she did would ever please him. Thankfully she'd learned that a long time ago and ignored his refusal to allow her to train as a surgeon. It had been hard when he'd kicked her out but she'd coped.

It had been hard too when he refused to walk her down the aisle because he disapproved of Mike and the 'weak' way he supported the rights of minorities and the underprivileged. Hard but no surprise. Tracey felt her careful, so as not to touch the cracks, steps growing slower. She'd better get a move on or she'd be late.

She forestalled his demand to know why she'd not come when he told her to by telling him about the operation.

"Worked did it, this transplant?"

"Yes. Yes it did. I had a call this morning to say she's doing well."

He didn't say he understood or forgave her but at least he didn't say his wishes were more important than a child's life.

Tracey checked her father's chart and told him his condition looked stable.

He nodded. That small action was his way of acknowledging her expertise. Not the first one either; it had been her he'd called after his fall. Whether it was as a doctor or a daughter she wasn't sure, but he'd wanted her then and had accepted her care and decision to call an ambulance without fuss. He'd not hesitated to name her as his next of kin and never in her hearing contradicted the nursing staff when they said how proud he must be of his daughter. Maybe the pain from his broken hip had shocked his heart into working emotionally as well as physically.

"I wanted to talk to you, Tracey. Explain. I know you think I was a bit strict with you when you were a child, but it was for your own good."

Strict? He'd bullied, threatened and demanded immediate unquestioning obedience. Tracey fiddled with his drip to give her time to gather her thoughts before replying. Maybe he really believed he'd acted in her best interests. Perhaps it had helped her career to know that however hard she tried sometimes it wasn't enough. Certainly the hours she'd spent alone in her room with nothing but school books for entertainment had helped her gain the grades to get into medical school. Could they even now grow close?

Tracey sat next to him and laid her hand over his. "That was a long time ago, Dad. Now it's my turn to look after you."

"That's right. You'll have to pack in your job now and come back home and nurse me."

"No, Dad. I promised to look after you and I will, but I'm also going to keep doing my job and remain living with my husband."

"I forbid it."

"You can't do that now, Dad."

"Oh can't I? How long do you think your career and that of your precious husband will last if I go to the papers? 'Top doctor and politician abandon father in his hour of need'."

As a result of Tracey's difficult childhood, although she still hoped for the best, she always prepared for the worst.

"We're not abandoning you, Dad. You can come and live with us in a separate flat and I'll hire someone to look after you. Mike has already released a press statement saying that. You don't have to accept our help of course, but if you refuse no one will believe it was never offered."

"I'll be lonely and miserable."

Just as she'd been as a child, but it couldn't have been any easier for him bringing her up alone and being incapable of giving or receiving love.

"Only if you choose to be. You can keep to yourself or join us anytime you like. If you do I'll take that as you accepting both my husband and my job. Again, it's your choice."

She watched him begin to reply, but his voice died away before he'd really said anything.

Tracey left. Her steps were no longer slow and deliberate. She strode out angrily hitting the cracks between the paving tiles as often as she missed them. She bumped into a heavily pregnant women.

"Sorry," Tracey murmured.

"No harm done. I expect you're rushing somewhere important."

"Actually no. I just wasn't paying attention."

"But, you are Doctor Rayner?"

"Yes. I'm sorry, I don't …"

"Lucia Cartwright. You …," she gestured to her heart.

"Lucia? No need to ask how you're getting on, you look wonderful. And you're pregnant!"

The women hugged and Lucia showed the baby scan she'd just had done. "You saved my life and now I'm creating a new one."

"The miracle of life."

"You're the miracle!"

Tracey couldn't help grinning as she walked away. Lucia

was so happy and she'd helped to make that possible. She wouldn't go so far as to call herself a miracle, but she was a good person. Dad might not be able to see it, or perhaps was just unwilling to admit it, but she knew for certain that giving in to his demands would be a disaster for her and still wouldn't earn his respect. She walked carefully again, this time making sure that every time her foot touched the floor it covered a crack.

She walked passed a room housing the scanner Mike had campaigned for. He was a good man too.

Another boost to her mood came when she went to check on her patient from the previous day. She was doing really well and all the indications were positive. The child gave her a cheeky grin and let go of her father's hand to give a thumbs up sign. The mother thanked Tracey profusely, but the father's words were all for his daughter, saying how he loved her and how proud he was of her.

Tracey had only just finished her rounds when her pager summoned her to the emergency theatre. Her incoming patient had suffered severe chest damage during a traffic accident. During a long and tiring operation Tracey and the team did all they could. The chances for this patient making a good recovery were slim, but Tracey told herself there was always hope.

As she dragged herself out of theatre she glanced at a sign pointing towards her father's ward. Yes, even in there was a heart she hoped would begin to work properly again. Dad's beat strongly enough, but that was the only use he put it to.

He'd be asleep now surely and she could creep in quietly without disturbing him. She'd done that the first few days after he'd been admitted. Tracey had sat with him and thought back to the past when Mum was still alive. Her death had robbed Tracey of two loving parents and left her with the angry shell of a man. He'd provided a safe home and had fed her and washed her clothes until she was old enough to take on those tasks. He bought her school uniform but never a ribbon for her hair. He took her to the dentist but not on picnics.

She sank down next to him and whispered, "I want my Dad back. He's been gone so long, but he's still in there. He must be."

Her tears splashed onto his hand resting on top of the blanket and she once again covered it with her own. "After your accident Mike took me to the park where you used to take me and Mum when I was little. The trees seem just as tall so I guess they've grown along with me. There are proper picnic benches there now. It won't be long until you're strong enough to walk to them from the car park." She blew her nose. "There would be nothing to stop you coming with us, but you never will. For one thing I could never ask and face the pain of your refusal."

As she stood to leave she thought she heard him say her name. "Dad, are you awake?"

He lifted his hand. As she touched it he held on. "I told her not to die. She loved me but she didn't obey. I needed you to be different."

"Oh, Dad."

"You're not though. You disobeyed me too."

"Yes, but I loved you too. Still love you."

He squeezed her hand.

"I'm sorry but I have to go. I've just been operating and the patient will be coming round now, that's if he ever does."

"Difficult one?"

"Very."

"You're a good doctor, everyone has been saying so. There must be hope."

"Yes, Dad there's always hope." Her job was to mend broken hearts and his was showing signs of recovery.

11. Heart In Her Handbag

Willian had been amazed when Della had agreed to go out with him. Nearly as amazed as he was at himself for having the nerve to ask her. Really he'd only done it to spite his mum. Or did he mean in spite of her? Aaaargh that woman! It seemed like her heart must be in the huge handbag he couldn't ever remember seeing her without. No emotion in her at all. Thank goodness William hadn't inherited her uncaring attitude. Usually he was relieved at that, but it did mean he felt every disappointment sharply.

His school friends and teachers had been thrilled when he was picked for the school's county tennis competition and he'd rushed home to tell Mum.

She just said, "Hardly Wimbledon is it?"

"No, but my teachers said this was a big step."

"Don't go getting your hopes up."

William won his match, but he didn't even try to get selected for the next level.

Later his teachers were impressed when he sat three exams a year early and passed them all. Mum had pointed out the B grade, not the two As. It had been like that his whole life. She'd battled so hard to feed and clothe him and provide a home that she didn't have energy left for a hug or word of praise.

A year ago she'd been telling him, as usual, how useless he was for not having a girlfriend.

"Are you expecting to stay living with me forever?"

"There is someone I like, but why would she want to go out with a no hoper like me?" William had asked.

"She said that?" Mum had seemed indignant at the idea someone else had taken on her role of running him down.

"No, I've not asked her."

"Then do it, you silly boy. Can't say yes if you don't ask can she?"

No, but neither could she say no and crush his hopes. And if she'd turned him down that could have made things awkward at work. Or maybe not. Della was lovely so probably got asked out quite often and would hardly notice his pitiful attempts.

Eventually he'd asked her, thinking at least her refusal might make Mum regret pushing him into it, but Della had seemed to bounce on the spot for a moment, then said yes. They'd been dating for almost a year now. He could still hardly believe his luck. Whenever she caught sight of him and ran to hug him, he really felt he was worth loving.

She'd dropped hints about meeting his family, but he wasn't risking that. He didn't want Mum pointing out all his flaws and for Della to see him for what he really was – nowhere near good enough for her.

"Why don't you ever bring that girlfriend of yours home?" Mum asked. "It's time you were getting married, or at least showing her you're serious about her and she won't think that if she hasn't been introduced to your family."

William tried to explain why he'd not brought Della home.

"Oh. Oh, yes, I see."

That just made him feel worse. Deep down he'd been

hoping she'd again tell him not to be silly, to say 'go and ask her'. If his own mother didn't think he was good enough for a girl she'd never met, obviously he wasn't.

William decided to stop tormenting himself. He'd finish with Della and free her to find someone worthy of her. They were sitting outside a bar, drinking coffee with William trying to find the words when Mum turned up.

"Aren't you going to introduce us, William?" she demanded.

Mum turned away as he did so and pulled a chair away from the next table. She sat facing Della.

"Now, young lady, you might not think my son is good enough for you, but let me tell you he is."

"I'm sure he is," Della said.

Mum ignored her and reached for that ever present handbag. "When I fell pregnant my parents warned me not to expect much from him. They said children of single parents were clingy and spoiled and had no ambition, but I've always done my best not to keep him dependent on me and to push him to achieve more and it paid off. Look at these."

She pulled a package from her bag and unfolded the protective cloth to reveal a mass of paperwork. There were photos of William, press clippings about his tennis matches, school reports, the slips notifying him of examination grades. William had thought she'd barely noticed anything he'd ever done, but she'd kept everything from the coloured badges he'd earned for reading in junior school, to the letter confirming his appointment at work.

"I've never once said how very, very proud I am of him, because I didn't know how and because I thought he must know. I see now I was wrong and that I should have done it."

Della leafed through the various documents, a smile on her face which grew broader the more she read.

William just stared at Mum. She was proud of him? She'd told Della he was good enough for her and, heavens, Della had agreed!

"So what do you say?" Mum demanded. "Are you going to marry him or not?"

William reached over and put a hand on Mum's arm. "Mum, she can't say yes. I haven't asked her yet."

"Oh. Right, I see. You get on with it then. I'll go and order champagne to celebrate."

William was amazed he could even speak after that. In fact for quite some time he couldn't, but eventually he got the words out.

"Yes," Della said. "Yes, yes, yes."

Just as well, as by then Mum was back with the waiter and champagne. As the wine was poured, William saw her slip the cork into her handbag along with all her other treasures.

12. You've Got To Be Kidding

Carrie dropped a teabag into what used to be her favourite mug and scowled at the animal face painted on it. She'd started to really hate goats. Not the animals themselves, they were as lovable and endearing as ever. It was all the ornaments, pictures, books, mugs, posters, stuffed toys and jigsaws that she was getting fed up with.

Carrie couldn't stand clutter. So much so that when friends first came to see her after she'd moved out of her parents' home, they'd glanced round her flat and said, "It'll look great when you've decorated." "You just need to buy a few bits and pieces to make it homely." Or "If you can't afford furnishings and ornaments after moving, I could lend you something."

"No need, this is it finished," Carrie had responded.

"But it's so empty!"

"Yes, it's lovely. I have everything I need and not a single thing more. Nothing to dust, no hunting through drawers of junk to find what I want, no moving three things to make room before I can put anything down."

Her once restfully tidy flat wasn't empty now, but stuffed with mostly useless goat shaped items. The madness had started after a holiday to Greece. Actually if she was honest, it had begun whilst she was there. The owners of the tiny hotel she'd stayed in had a goat to provide milk. Carrie had been shown how to milk it and had walked it so it could munch the plants along the roadside. Maybe an odd way to spend a holiday, certainly the hotel owner had seemed to think so, but for someone who'd always lived in a city it had been a welcome novelty. It wasn't just tending the goat she'd enjoyed, but the simplicity of life in the Greek village. No internet, no shops but the twice weekly market, no traffic. Bliss. If she could afford it she'd go back like a shot.

The only thing she'd missed was her mug of tea in the morning. The hotel provided fragrant coffee, but it came in those pots with a plunger. Despite it not being Carrie who had to measure out the grounds and then wash everything clean afterwards, it all seemed too much of a faff to her. Tea was so much easier. Drop in a bag, pour on water, swish it round and bung it in the bin. All done.

Carrie had come home with a renewed appreciation of her favourite drink and a love of goat's cheese. She'd taken photos of the goat, one of which became her screensaver at work and she'd bought herself a ceramic version of the creature as a souvenir. That one tiny impulse to own something unnecessary had been Carrie's downfall. Since then for every birthday and Christmas people gave her something involving goats. Models of goats in a variety of materials from a tiny one in solid silver to an almost life sized fluffy version were in the majority, but there were plenty of other versions. Sweatshirts embroidered with goats, books about goats, bags with goats decorating them, a goat shaped cover for her phone. She just didn't need or want all that stuff. But if someone had taken the trouble to find what they thought would be a cherished gift she felt obliged to try to appreciate, or at least seem to. So much of her life was taken up with remembering which mug to use when her brother popped round, which cushion to recline against when her best friend Sue visited. She'd considered losing the lot in a fire but that wouldn't be fair to the neighbours, it was dangerous, illegal and if the insurance company didn't pay up she'd be homeless.

She did try to put a stop to it. When she thought she could get away with it she donated some of the gifts to charity shops. When asked what she'd like for her birthday she said, "I'm so lucky to have everything I need and friends who want to give me more, but honestly I'd rather you didn't go to a lot of trouble and expense."

Her friends clubbed together to buy three real life goats! Not ones she'd need to get up to the seventh floor, but animals which would provide much needed milk to a poor family in a village in Zambia. Carrie rather liked that idea. The goats would be valuable and therefore well treated and the family would benefit too. Plus there was the option to receive messages by email instead of post so she could enjoy the updates and pictures without them taking up space. That solution wouldn't work every year though. Her friends and family wanted to give her something for herself, not to strangers, however needy they might be. And to be honest, Carrie quite liked receiving gifts, just not ones involving goats or which cluttered up her flat. Something nice, luxurious even, but quickly used and disposed of would be ideal. Not chocolates though as she struggled with her weight and not toiletries as her skincare was as minimal as the rest of her life. Wash, dry, done.

She realised she was difficult to buy for. The only way to deter people from buying her more goat stuff was to ask for something else. As she tried to think, she made herself another mug of tea. Ah! Teabags. Carrie usually bought the shop's own brand ones. They were fine, but far nicer, more expensive varieties were available. When she next went shopping, she noted the most indulgent looking brand. Perfect; they were even Fair trade so it wasn't just Carrie who'd benefit. Teabags keep for ages too, so it didn't matter at all that almost everyone she knew bought her a large pack for Christmas.

At least, it didn't matter to Carrie. Her friends and family didn't seem so pleased.

"But these are exactly what I want and I have enough here to last me until my next birthday."

She'd hoped they'd take that as a hint to repeat the gift, but apparently teabags weren't special enough for a big birthday.

"But it isn't. Twenty-one and forty could be considered milestones, but not thirty. There's nothing special about being thirty."

"Of course there is and as you never make a fuss of yourself, I'm going to organise a party for you," said her friend Sue.

"Please, don't go to any…"

"Don't worry, I don't mean a disco or anything completely not you. I thought a nice tea party in our garden. We can eat cake, drink tea and chat."

"Oh. Thank you. That does sound nice."

It was too. Very relaxed, with guests each bringing a plate of cakes or cookies. Every one of her friends and most of her family and colleagues turned up. The weather was kind; sunny but not too hot to enjoy the tea.

Oh but the presents! There was a mountain of them. Each was a different size and shape and all were beautifully wrapped. It was so kind of people, but Carrie really wished they hadn't bothered, especially once she began unwrapping them. There were tea cups, trays and caddies, special spoons, strainers and cloths. Anything you could think of to do with tea was there, many of the items also decorated with images of goats. Quite a few items were identical to those she'd taken to the charity shops just a few weeks previously in an attempt to provide room for the things she'd guessed she would be given. Even so, she didn't have space for all this lot. There was even a tea pot in the shape of a goat, which was far too large and heavy for Carrie to ever use.

Carrie's face hurt from the effort of giving a brilliantly happy smile as she unwrapped each carefully chosen and totally unwanted item. "So generous, you really shouldn't have." It was worth it, everyone looked so happy.

Actually they looked a bit too happy. Exactly as though they were trying not to laugh.

"Got you!" her brother said. "You don't really want all this stuff, do you?"

"Umm, well I …"

"Good thing it was all cheap then. We've been scouring charity shops and car boot sales for weeks. If you like, I can load it all in my car and drop it off at Oxfam tomorrow?"

"If you really don't mind?"

"We don't," Sue said. "We finally realised you don't like junk, clutter and bits and pieces even if they are cute or pretty."

"I don't. Sorry. I suppose it's my fault for not saying so in the first place."

"To be fair, you did try. We just didn't listen because we couldn't think what you'd really like. I hope we've got it right this time." She handed Carrie an envelope.

Carefully Carrie opened it and took out the slip of paper inside. It was a travel voucher. One large enough to pay for a trip to Greece.

"I don't know what to say."

"Don't say anything, just send us a postcard," Sue said.

Her brother added, "But don't buy us any souvenirs featuring goats. We've all had quite enough of those!"

13. Best Thing In The World

"It's the best thing in the world," Kelly gushed into her phone.

I'd no idea what was so good, but could predict her response if I asked. She'd roll her eyes and say, "Don't know much, do you, Nan?"

That sounds cheeky. It is, but only a little. It's just a phrase and she knows I know that. It's the same with 'the best thing in the world'. That's just a phrase, not to be taken seriously. Last week the best thing was white chocolate… And rollerblading, Dr Who, jambalaya made by her other gran and Saturday mornings.

Even so, I wanted her to say it about me, or just something connected with me. The closest I ever got was, "You're alright, Nan." She said that a lot, was always happy to spend time with me, she confided in me and we laughed together. That should have been more than enough…

I guess I was a little insecure, what with not being what some would call her real gran. Toby, my son, is the only father Kelly's ever known, but her mother was already pregnant when they met. I'll admit I had reservations at the time, but it's all worked out much better than I could have hoped. Kelly is coming up to fifteen now and I love her so much that no blood tie could make me care any more.

"What is it this time?" I asked, when she finally ended her call. "What's the new best thing in the world?"

She didn't roll her eyes. Instead she produced a knitted

hat. "Brills, isn't it?"

It was big, mad and colourful. Totally right for her and beautifully made. I guessed who by and a stab of jealousy shot through me. It shouldn't have. Kelly's other gran is a talented lady, but so am I in different ways. We get along fine and Kelly described us both as "alright". Knitting though was proper granny stuff.

"It's lovely," I declared truthfully. "She's very clever, your other gran."

"Totally is. She got this on eBay for a fiver."

I felt better at that, and suggested we go for an ice cream, so she could show it off. "The Bluebird does a lemon meringue one."

"Great call, Nan. That's the best flavour in the world!"

I'd thought it was going to be my moment. The one when something connected with me was the best thing in the world. They'd sold out.

"Doesn't matter. The coconut one is great," Kelly said. She ate enthusiastically, but didn't say the magic words.

"Hi, Kells," said a teenage boy. "Nice hat."

She blushed and tried to hide behind the cone.

"So, that's him?" I asked when he was out of earshot. "The boy you have a crush on?"

"Yeah, that's Ian but it's way more than a crush."

"He's the best thing in the world?" I guessed.

"Noooo! Ian, well… he's alright, you know?"

"Alright is better than the best thing in the world?"

"Oh, Nan, you don't know much do you?"

"Actually, young lady, I know everything I'll ever need to know."

14. Baked Well

"Could you do something for Aidan's birthday?" Clara's husband asked her.

They'd already bought the boy's present, so Alex must mean a celebration of some kind. "I'm not sure he'll want a party, but if he does I'll organise one," Clara said.

Of course she would. She held girly parties for her two daughters on their birthdays, so it was only right she make the same effort for Alex's son. She'd thrown one for her youngest soon after he'd come to live with them. On that occasion Aidan had abruptly presented his gift, taken some food and holed up in his bedroom. Clara couldn't blame him. Not many twelve-year-old boys wanted to attend the frothy parties of girls half their age. One like Aidan certainly wouldn't and didn't have the life skills to pretend.

"Thanks. And could you make a big Bakewell tart?" Alex asked. "Last time you did little ones he said they were his favourite, because of the pattern on top."

Of course she'd make his favourite and never mind if his reason for preferring it wasn't people's usual reason for having a favourite type of cake.

Aidan made it clear he didn't want a party at home, nor to go out anywhere to celebrate his birthday. Clara wasn't surprised – large groups of people and unfamiliar places, especially if they were noisy, made him uncomfortable.

"How about inviting a few friends for tea?" She named two boys who'd been to the house before.

Aidan agreed with an air of doing her a favour.

When the girls realised she was making their stepbrother's birthday cake, they wanted to help. Getting the equipment and ingredients together took hardly any longer than usual with their assistance. Clara let them take turns beating the sugar and butter together. That was actually helpful as she tended to skimp on that stage. They were enthusiastic mixers. So much so that she had to restrain them as the other ingredients were incorporated for fear more would end up on the walls than in the tin. Thankfully the recipe didn't call for gentle folding in.

She double-checked the instructions; with so much help it was easy to get distracted. Clara rolled out her pastry and lined a large flat baking tray. It's always tricky, even without an audience, to get such a large piece of pastry rolled evenly and in the tin without damage.

As instructed, the girls carefully pricked the pastry all over with a fork.

"Why do we do that, Mum?" the older one asked.

"So the cake stays nice and level and doesn't have a soggy bottom!"

They giggled over the soggy bottom, but agreed solemnly that getting it level was important for Aidan.

They spread the raspberry jam onto the pastry, but not until after it had been sieved. He didn't like 'bits' and raspberry seeds certainly counted as that. Clara was glad of her helpers relieving her of that tedious task.

The girls spooned in the almond sponge mixture, which Clara smoothed level. She placed the cake in the oven at the correct temperature and started the timer. She wanted to turn the tin halfway through to ensure it cooked evenly.

After the girls helped wash up they wanted to ice the cake.

"Not yet. It needs to cool for a long time." That was true.

It was also the case that icing it was a fiddly task which would be easier without them. Just like Aidan's mother apparently found life easier without him. Once Clara and Alex married, his mother decided Aidan was better off with his dad and in a family with other children.

Aidan was a little different and could be difficult to cope with. It wasn't deliberate, he just needed some things done a particular way, or in a particular order. He'd be upset if asked to put on his coat before his shoes. Pouring sauce or gravy over his food distressed him. He needed to do it himself, so it went in the right place. Mostly it was little things and easy to accommodate once Clara knew he had a preference.

He dressed himself in the 'right' order. Unpacked his school bag every night and the following morning put everything back in the 'right' order. Aidan was good at organising himself. If Clara told him to be ready to leave at a particular time then he would be – and wonder why she and the girls weren't!

He had rituals, so it was hard to hurry him. No, not hard, impossible. If he missed a step he'd have to start again. If he was prevented from doing so there would be something approaching a tantrum. Aidan tended to keep his emotions hidden, and couldn't properly control them once they were let out.

She'd maybe been too harsh towards his mother. How difficult for everyone it must have been when he was too young to do much for himself and wasn't able to communicate how he needed things to be done in order to keep him calm and comfortable.

When it was time to ice the cake Clara had the kitchen to herself. The others, all four of them, were on a walk through the woods. Aidan enjoyed such trips. He liked looking at a map to plan the best route. No one, possibly not Aidan himself, knew why one particular route was right one day and taking a different path better on other occasions, but as everybody else was happy to wander wherever he suggested that was no problem. The girls thought he was clever to find different paths. They gave him all the credit for every bird, butterfly and flower they saw, which did his confidence good. Aidan liked the peace of the woods. The quiet soothed him so much he tolerated the girls interrupting it to show him their finds. He was learning to compromise.

Life was like that, wasn't it? Making compromises. Not with Aidan's cake though, Clara wanted it to be perfect. Alex had helped her turn it out of the tin, so she could support it with a tea towel stretched taut over the sponge top. There was a second when she thought it might stick but it came away beautifully and was positioned perfectly on the serving tray. She'd have to ice it in situ as it would be impossible to move without damage once that was done.

Once the rest of the family were on their walk, Clara made two batches of icing. One pure white for the base, one deep brown for the feathering. The white was poured on and teased to the edges with a silicone spatula. Slowly, slowly so as not to incorporate cake crumbs which would spoil the look. Straight away she picked up the plastic bag, spooned in the brown icing and began to lay it over the white in long, thin strips. One longways, right down the centre, first. There was probably a technical names for that. Transverse was it? Aidan would know.

Parallel to the first she laid a line along the edge of the tart, then the same on the other side. The trick was to pretend confidence and do it as though nothing could go wrong. Stop to think, hesitate for any reason, and she'd get a wiggle in the line. There was no way of correcting such a mistake. The two colour icings couldn't be separated without leaving a stain and even if they could it would be too late. The entire operation had to be completed before the white began to set.

Clara continued with the lines until they ran evenly down the entire cake. Longitudinally, was that it? She was almost certain it was.

There was no time to admire her neatness and precision as the next step couldn't wait. With a butter knife she dragged through the two layers of icing. First going left to right, then right to left across the cake at right angles to the brown lines. It was easy really, just as long as she worked fast, applied exactly enough pressure to go through the icing, but not touch the cake, and remembered to wipe the knife clean on every pass. It was tempting to save time by doing it only after crossing in one direction, and that would be OK, but risked her forgetting, accumulating too much icing on the knife and getting a lump or smudge. It was best to trust the ritual of doing it every time. It was comforting and safe. No wonder Aidan clung to his.

The result was good. Really good. The best she'd ever done, certainly for one of that size. Usually she made individual tarts. They gave room for error – if she messed one up she ate it and still had enough for a full plate at tea time.

Good as it was, the cake wasn't right for Aidan. The pastry edges weren't precisely, shop-bought, even. There was nothing wrong with them really, but they were what Aidan would see. He wouldn't make a fuss, not if he was having a good day and she was sure he would be, but they'd spoil his pleasure in the cake.

Clara took a sharp knife and cut away the pastry edges, taking as little of the cake as possible. Perfect! Except the exposed edges of cake would dry out by tomorrow. She needed to cover them. Chocolate, as is so often the case, was the answer.

She melted some of her stash, beat in butter and icing sugar until she had just the right consistency to pipe all around the cake. It looked pretty good, but wasn't quite finished. Clara intended to top alternate stars of chocolate icing with white chocolate drops and cherries. One to match the white icing and one the jam. The neatness of that would please Aidan.

Clara quickly rinsed and halved glacé cherries and put them in place. The chocolate drops were more of a problem. The packs had been in and out the cupboard so often as she used other baking ingredients that the little points had broken off some, making them all look dusty. The chocolate was fine, she tried a few to reassure herself on that point, but they looked scruffy.

Alex came in as she was melting them down. "We got a bit muddy, so Aidan and the girls are cleaning our boots in the garage." He snaffled an offcut of pastry edge. "Gorgeous."

"It's nice to be appreciated."

"I meant the cake… Although obviously you're gorgeous too. Is that chocolate on your nose?"

"It'll be icing."

"Ah. What are you doing now?" Alex asked.

"Making chocolate drops to go between the cherries."

"That'll look nice." He picked up a bag she'd discarded onto the table. "You're melting down chocolate drops to make chocolate drops?"

"It's not as mad as it sounds. I'm making better ones."

"For Aidan, for my son?"

"Of course."

"I can't tell you how much I love you."

"You can try showing me later… and now by keeping the children away, so I can finish this and hide it."

"I'll do that. And I'll help a bit more with some tidying up." He grabbed a few more offcuts and stuffed them in his mouth.

Aidan's birthday went well. He politely thanked Alex and Clara for the weather station he'd requested and seemed pleased with the notebooks his stepsisters gave him. His mum rang just before school to wish him a happy birthday. She'd sent a gift voucher. Clara reminded herself that something wasn't necessarily wrong just because it was easy.

Loving Alex and her girls was easy. Agreeing that Aidan should come and live with them had been easy too. Easy because what choice did she have? Learning to adjust to his idiosyncrasies, whilst not disrupting everyone else's lives, hadn't been easy at all, but she'd managed pretty well.

Aidan's school friends came home with him. Aidan smiled when he saw the cake. It wasn't a polite smile to make her feel good. Aidan didn't know how to do that. It was a smile of genuine pleasure. The cake didn't last long, but she'd made it to be eaten, not just admired. Afterwards the boys took more food up to Aidan's room and stayed there until it was time for them to leave.

When they'd gone, Aidan brought down the used plates. "Thank you for making that cake for my birthday. It's my favourite kind."

"Well, that's lucky."

"No it isn't." Aidan smiled again, a big grin just like his dad's. "You knew."

"Yes. Yes I did." It had been quite a lot of work, but the cake, just like the boy, was worth the effort.

15. An Imaginative Boy

"Can I have some food please, Mum?" Mathew asked after school on Friday.

"Of course. What would you like?"

"It's not for me."

"Oh? For your friend again?" He'd asked the same thing that morning. Cherryl thought he'd just wanted to share a treat and gave him a packet of biscuits to take to school.

Mathew nodded.

"Which one?" Was the poor boy's family reliant on food banks? Cherryl sometimes put a tin into the supermarket collecting box, but assumed the people who needed them were all strangers.

Mathew fidgeted. "He didn't want me to tell."

That was understandable, but made it harder to help. Cherryl opened the cupboards, looking for suitable items. "Would you like to invite him round for tea this weekend?" she asked, hoping her son wouldn't see that as betraying a confidence.

"He doesn't want to come in and you can't see him, Mum."

"Ah!" An imaginary friend. Cherryl humoured her son by giving him a couple of cereal bars. "I know he'll like these."

Mathew had always been a picky eater, but lately he'd taken a liking for the chewy snacks and they provided a bit more nutrition than the chocolate and chips which were about the only other things he'd eat without a fuss.

"Great!" Mathew took the cereal bars and rushed outside.

Cherryl smiled at his enthusiasm, but couldn't help wondering what had caused Mathew to invent a companion. Imaginary friends weren't unusual, especially with an only child, but Mathew had never mentioned one before and at eight seemed a bit old to start.

When he came back in, she probed gently and was reassured by his answers. It seemed he was perfectly happy at school, had plenty of friends and hadn't suffered any unsettling experiences.

"Can I eat it in my den?" he asked when she gave him his tea.

"Go on then."

When Mathew had wanted a treehouse, his big cousin Karl had helped him and Cherryl's husband convert the garden shed into a 'secret' den. That involved getting rid of the junk, painting the outside with a camouflage pattern, fixing up blinds and making it cosy with spare pillows, scruffy cushions and the padding from their old sun loungers. Mathew and his cousins had shared picnics in there whenever Cherryl's sister Rachel had come to visit.

That hadn't happened for a while. Was missing his cousins the reason Mathew had invented a friend? Whatever the cause, Cherryl was going to handle the situation tactfully. She knew only too well how saying the wrong thing could upset a sensitive child. Or a not so sensitive adult come to that. Cherryl and her sister had fallen out on numerous occasions as children. Rachel was stubborn; if she thought she was right about something, anyone presenting a different point of view was considered the enemy. Even so, Cherryl couldn't always make herself stay quiet if she thought her sister was making a mistake.

"You're far too strict with your kids," she'd said, when instead of letting them go straight out to play in Mathew's den she'd insisted the younger one finish his homework and the older lad revise for his final GCSE.

"Easy for you to say," Rachel had snapped. "Now their dad has cleared off with that woman, I can't leave the discipline up to him."

That was unfair. Cherryl's husband worked away a lot, so she had to be the one to tell Mathew off, or insist he do something, on the rare occasions that was needed and she didn't shirk the responsibility. "You were just as strict with them before Grant left and anyway, now he's not there you should be showing them some love and support."

"Letting them have their way all the time like your precious Mathew, you mean."

They'd fallen out over it and, despite Cherryl's attempts to contact Rachel, they'd not spoken for months. Cherryl's information about Rachel and the children was now secondhand; passed on by her parents and mutual friends. The last Cherryl heard the eldest child had got great GCSE results and been accepted into college and the youngest was in line for a Duke of Edinburgh award for something chemistry related. It seemed Rachel was making a far better job of raising her kids than Cherryl had given her credit for.

Cherryl tried calling her sister. Her mobile was engaged. When she tried the landline, as usual the answering machine kicked in. Seeing her son pushing open the kitchen door, Cherryl hung up.

He was holding an empty plate. It was possible he'd eaten the entire meal, but that would be unusual.

"Mathew, if there was anything you couldn't eat, please

put it in the bin. It's not good to leave food outside." She was worried about attracting rats, but didn't want to discourage him from playing outdoors.

"There's nothing left," he said, with a certainty which convinced Cherryl. "Can my friend have a glass of milk?"

"Shall I pour it for him?"

"I can do it. And can he have another cereal bar? He's really hungry."

"No, but if he's as hungry as you say maybe he'd like some fruit or vegetables?"

"Shall I ask him?"

"You do that. If he says yes, help yourself to anything from the fruit bowl or salad crisper in the fridge."

"Thanks, Mum!" Mathew rushed off returning a few seconds later for the milk, which he carefully carried outside.

On Saturday, bananas and oranges vanished from the fruit bowl and the stock of carrots became seriously depleted. Maybe the imaginary friend would be be a good influence on Mathew's diet?

"Mum, can my friend have some clothes?" was Mathew's next request.

"He can borrow yours, love."

"They won't fit. He's bigger than me."

Fortunately a charity bag had been pushed through the door recently. Cherryl had sorted through the wardrobe and found a few items of hers and her husband's they were unlikely to wear again.

"Have a look in there to see if there's anything of your dad's which will do."

"Thanks, Mum." He rushed out into the garden, like Santa ready to deliver gifts.

He spent most of Saturday in the garden shed, which pleased Cherryl. Mathew's electronic games were all educational ones, but she hadn't really liked him spending so long playing on them.

When Cherryl began to prepare the evening meal, she discovered there was no salad left. If Mathew had already eaten the mixed leaves, cucumber and radishes it was OK for him to have nothing but chips with his tea, but it wouldn't do her waistline any good.

"You said I could help myself," Mathew said when she mentioned it.

She had, she remembered. Cherryl also recalled her sister's fury when Rachel's oldest boy had used all his mum's dried fruit, nuts and spices for a school art project. That included a gift pack of slender vanilla pods, intricate star anise and ultra expensive saffron which Cherryl had given her for Christmas, so she could understand Rachel being upset.

The field of sunflowers he'd created looked, and smelled, amazing. Cherryl felt he should have been praised for producing such a lovely piece of art, not just berated for wasting cooking ingredients. The poor lad hadn't shown his mum a single piece of artwork since, though she'd said the teachers praised his creativity in parents' evenings.

Cherryl didn't know if Rachel had learned from that incident, but she certainly had. It was odd that using his imagination seemed to be increasing Mathew's appetite, but there was no way she would stifle his creativity as her sister did with her sons.

That evening Mathew showered and brushed his teeth

without prompting.

"My friend says it's horrible to be all dirty."

"He's right. It's very important to wash properly and look after your teeth."

The imaginary friend really was a good influence Cherryl told herself, and her husband when he called home that night. She changed her mind on Sunday when she discovered a bar of soap, toothbrush and toothpaste had been taken from the bathroom.

If Cherryl didn't want to worry Mathew, or make him clam up, she must tread carefully. Perhaps if she, very gently, revealed the friend didn't exist, Mathew would realise he didn't have to take things from the house in order to play his game?

"Maybe he'd like to come in and use our shower?" she suggested when Mathew confessed to taking the toiletries for his friend.

"I don't know…"

"I won't mind, not if he's your friend."

"I'll ask him." Mathew headed for the garden, but much more slowly than he had over the rest of the weekend.

Cherryl was becoming a little worried about what was going on in Mathew's head. Rachel used to worry about her boys' imaginations too and Cherryl had said not to, and instead let them be children. In effect she'd criticised Rachel for caring about her boys. Feeling bad about that Cherryl decided to leave yet another message asking if they could patch things up.

To Cherryl's amazement, Rachel answered her call. Because of the surprise and Rachel being obviously upset it was difficult to understand her words.

"… message saying my call can't be connected. I should have stopped him going," Rachel continued.

"Who are you talking about?" Cherryl asked.

"Karl. I thought he was staying with a friend, but he's run away. Or maybe been kidnapped."

"Kidnapped?" That seemed farfetched.

"He's not taken any clothes. I checked just now, after he didn't answer his phone, and found great files of artwork. It's brilliant and… " she started to cry.

"Rachel, take a really deep breath."

Cherryl heard her gulp in air.

"He said he didn't want to study engineering, but do art instead. He threatened to leave home if I insisted. We rowed… He'd been going to stay with his friend for a few days, so when he stormed off carrying his rucksack I thought that's where he was going. It seemed better to let him, than try dragging him back."

"You did the right thing. I expect he really is with his friend and will have calmed down by now."

"Maybe." Rachel herself sounded much calmer now.

"And, if he wants to do art and his work is brilliant, maybe…?"

"I thought it was just an excuse to get out of doing homework, but he's obviously spent a lot of time on it and the teachers who've being saying he had talent are right. I didn't know… I thought he was kidding himself. Ironic isn't it? I complained about his imagination and now I'm imagining the worst has happened to him."

The kitchen door opened. Cherryl looked up to see her son ushering his big cousin into the house.

"Karl is fine. He's right…" Seeing her nephew's look of

alarm, she continued, "Maybe he just forgot to charge his phone. I'm sure he'll call you as soon as he can. I'd better go so he can get through."

"Was that my mum?" Karl asked as soon as Cherryl ended the call.

"She's worried sick. You should call her."

He shook his head. "You were right about my phone being flat. Anyway, she never listens to me."

"Something tells me she will this time." Cherryl indicated the charger on the hall table. "Plug your phone in there, then have a shower and use that famous imagination of yours to think what you'll say."

To Mathew she said, "It's OK, love. Either he'll be going home tonight, or he can stay in the spare room. Why don't you go and get his stuff from the shed?"

As soon as she was alone again, Cherryl rang Rachel. "Karl is safe."

"Where? What's happened? How do you know?"

"I'm sure he'll tell you if you listen to him."

"I will. I promise I will. I'll listen to you too. You were right, I didn't have enough faith in his imagination."

"None of us are perfect. I think I've had too much faith in Mathew's. But everything's going to be OK."

Mathew came back in then, carrying Karl's rucksack. "I think he's still hungry, Mum. Can you make him some tea?"

"Of course. What do you think he'd like? More salad?"

"No, chips!"

Cherryl smiled, relieved that everything had returned to normal.

16. Flashbacks

Sam's earliest memory was of his big brother Paul saying there were no monsters under his bed.

"There are, there are," Sam insisted.

"They're only in your head," Paul reassured him. "Be brave and stand up to them and they'll be gone forever."

Paul held his hand as they knelt by the bed and peered underneath. At first Sam saw scary shapes but, as Paul urged him to stay still, his eyes adjusted and the monsters dissolved into nothing more than dust and shadows.

"You scared them away," Sam said.

"We did it together."

Knowing his brother was looking out for him helped Sam to be brave, right until Paul explained he'd be leaving. Then Sam had felt vulnerable and allowed himself to be drawn into a gang of local lads who hung about the estate causing trouble.

"You'd be better off keeping away from them and concentrating on your schoolwork," Paul warned when he found out.

"They're OK," Sam said. He couldn't explain that he'd joined because being one of them was the only way he could see to avoid becoming one of their victims.

"I hear you've been teasing Arthur Black," Paul said the next time he came back home.

"Who?" Sam knew who Paul meant. Arthur Black was as

old as Sam's parents, but did schoolboy jobs like a paper round in the morning and filling shelves in the corner shop in the evening. Often he acted like a scared kid too. He was known as Rocket because some idiot had let off a firework in the shop while he was working. The shop owner had gone totally ballistic and fair enough. It was a stupid and dangerous thing to do. Even Sam was nowhere near daft enough for that.

Arthur Black didn't get angry, instead he'd dived inside the deep freeze and sobbed. When they got him out, rocket shaped ice lollies were stuck to him where he'd wet himself. He'd been nervy even before that, jumping in alarm whenever a car backfired or there was any unexpected noise, but he was worse afterwards. Getting a reaction from Rocket was the main source of entertainment for the gang.

"It's just a laugh. Everyone does it," Sam said.

"A laugh?" Paul looked so angry Sam put his hands up ready to defend himself.

Paul didn't hit him, instead he pointed out, "It isn't so funny if you're the one being bullied, and 'everyone does it' is no excuse."

Sam remembered the 'games' the gang played with him before he'd agreed to join. "Suppose not."

He still did it though. Had to really. You either did what the rest of the gang wanted or you were on your own. Sam didn't actually make loud bangs as Rocket walked by, but he laughed as hard as the others whenever anyone else did. To see and hear a grown man yell and run because someone had dropped a dustbin lid wasn't really funny, but it stopped Sam and his friends having to confront their own fears for the future.

On their estate it was more common for people to go to

prison than out to work. Some got jobs, but they didn't stick around. It was a bit different with Paul as he didn't move out thinking he was better than the rest of them. He joined the army and went away for training and then on tours of duty. He always came back though.

Paul stayed with his family when on leave, but he always spent some time with Rocket. Sam was jealous. He wanted to show off his big, brave brother to his new mates. He liked to see the respect in their eyes and feel a little of it transfer to him.

"Teach me some army stuff so I know what to do when I join up," Sam pleaded.

"You'd be better off doing your homework," Paul told him. "You'll have more options for what to do after school if you pass your exams and you're bright enough to do it if you try."

"That stuff is boring."

"Do it anyway. I'll read it through when I come back from Arthur's."

"Same regiment," Paul said when Sam asked his brother why he bothered visiting a coward like Rocket. "And he's done things I'm not sure I could, and hope I never have to find out."

It took Sam a long time to work out what Paul really meant and why he cared. It took him even longer to realise Rocket was no coward.

"Why didn't you say?" he asked Paul.

"Because the answer is something kids like you should never have to understand."

Sam didn't, not really. Not until his brother's latest return from duty. Then it was just his body. Paul wasn't dead, but it seemed to Sam that his brother wasn't really there. Sometimes he stared at nothing with the same empty look Sam had seen in Rocket's eyes. Post traumatic stress disorder, the doctors said.

He had counselling and gradually the old Paul began to reappear. But a door slamming or firework going off could make him crumble. When reports of fighting came onto the news he'd stare at the screen. Sam knew he wasn't watching that battle, but the one he'd been involved in and wouldn't talk about. He wondered what it was that Rocket heard and saw whenever the gang of kids decided to make themselves feel brave by frightening him.

When Paul's medal was presented, Sam saw the strong, heroic brother he'd idolised. The family went out for a meal afterwards to celebrate. They'd just clinked their glasses of wine, coke and beer when a waiter dropped a metal tray. Everyone jumped a bit and looked around. Everyone but Paul. He dived under the table. Sam looked down at him and for a moment the big brave brother and frightened little kid seemed to have swapped places.

Sam bent down with a fork in his hand and acted though he'd just picked it up. "You looking for this?" he said.

Probably nobody was fooled, but Paul nodded and allowed Sam to pull him to his feet and everyone was able to carry on with their meal as though nothing had happened. Sam knew right then that he wouldn't be following his brother into the army. He wasn't as brave as Paul and Arthur Black. That didn't mean he had to live like a coward.

After school the next day someone in the gang suggested, "Let's go over the flats and wind up Rocket."

"No," Sam said.

"What, you scared?"

"There's nothing brave about seven lads frightening one old man and running away. It's no fun either."

Some of the boys looked uncomfortable. One demanded, "You gonna stop us?"

"How can I? I'm going back to mine to do my homework." Sam walked away, forcing himself not to run even when he heard rapid footsteps behind him.

The other boys yelled insults, but they didn't come after him. Sam didn't look back, but he was sure if he had he'd have seen nothing but dust and shadows.

17. Cheerful Denial

Veronica spotted Sally heading in her direction, and hastily made her escape. OK, so hiding in the stationery cupboard was a bit silly, but it was the best she could think of at short notice. It worked, after calling her name a couple of times Sally gave up. When Veronica returned to the main office she had the place to herself.

Usually Veronica ate her sandwiches at her desk, but whenever Sally was in work she'd try to coax her out.

"There's a lovely little tea shop I pass on my way to work. Would you like to try it with me?" Sally had asked a while back.

"I've brought my lunch with me," Veronica told her, tapping the plastic box on her work station to emphasise the point.

"Ah, right." Then after a moment added, "It's a lovely day. How about I grab something from the deli and we eat lunch in the park then?"

"It would set my hay fever off. You go though. Some fresh air might do you good, you look a bit peaky."

"Right, OK. I will then."

On various occasions Sally had suggested walking by the river, looking round the shops and even visiting the library in their lunch hour to research Johnny Depp. When Veronica had, reasonably politely, rebuffed every single idea which involved leaving the office Sally said, "Do you fancy ordering in a pizza and doing the crossword together?"

"No, Sally I do not. I fancy being left alone to eat my sandwich in peace and to get on with some work."

Veronica had concentrated on her spreadsheets to avoid seeing the hurt which she knew would be on Sally's face. Although Veronica didn't really want to be rude it seemed that was the only way Sally would take the hint and stop trying to make friends. Thankfully she now only worked part time.

When Veronica had joined the company about a year previously, Sally had been a full time admin assistant and hadn't seemed too bad. Actually she'd seemed lovely back then. She'd helped Veronica settle in and they'd chatted about TV programmes they'd seen and debated the various merits of the hunky leading men. Veronica had thought she'd found the friend she so badly needed. Then Sally had cut her hours and started doing something at one of the local hospitals on the days she didn't come in to the office. Veronica had assumed she worked there, perhaps on reception or something, but made it very clear she didn't want to know anything about it.

Sally, obligingly, didn't say anything more to her on the subject, but she did talk to the others now and then. Veronica couldn't help overhearing about the lovely staff, digital TV she watched from a nice soft chair and about the free coffee machine. She began to suspect Sally didn't actually work there at all but was a volunteer. One who spent most of her time socialising in the staffroom whilst kidding herself she was helping out. Veronica shuddered as she imagined Sally jollying along the patients by telling them how lucky they were to have her to talk to and trying to turn every negative into a positive. Telling them that life was precious and how important it was to make the most of every minute, and all those other empty clichés.

That's when Veronica had started trying to avoid her. The last thing Veronica needed was to spend time with someone else who was relentlessly cheerful, so determined to look on the bright side. Sally reminded her too much of Mum. They were both wrong. Life was rubbish sometimes and no amount of pretending otherwise would change that. Mum might smile through the worry, but Veronica just couldn't.

"I'm so lucky I spotted the lump early," Mum said. "At least I haven't lost my hair," was another favourite refrain until it came out in clumps. Mum just laughed and said, "Think of the money I'm saving on dye covering the grey."

The fact that she was required to drink extra fluid after treatments, to move the drugs through her body, was seen as a good thing as it was an excuse to stop at a tea shop on the way home. Mum acted as though that was a treat rather than yet another medical inconvenience. Veronica had to bite her tongue and keep her distance to avoid yelling that Mum might well have lots of luck, but it was all bad.

Mum was grateful for anything and everything. The kindness of ladies from the local bingo club who took it in turns to accompany her to hospital and the free bus passes which meant it cost them nothing but time. For neighbours who called in whilst Veronica was at work to see she had everything she needed.

She was even grateful for the things Veronica did to keep her distance, save her having to look into Mum's eyes or hearing the occasional tremble in her voice. Long shopping trips and dropping Mum off to visit friends or play bingo whenever she was strong enough. Renting all her favourite films and looking through photo albums.

"It's such fun to share my past with you, love." There was never a mention that there may not be a future and that Veronica refused to acknowledge the present.

When Mum's treatment was moved to another hospital further away Mum just said it would be a nice change to go somewhere else and checked the bus timetable. Even Mum looked a little daunted when she realised how long and complicated the journey would be.

Veronica took a huge steadying breath. "I'll drive you." The drive itself would be little trouble and her boss would be understanding about the time off. In fact she'd sometimes mentioned that Veronica worked longer hours than she was paid for. What worried Veronica was that she'd have to face up to Mum's illness, hear details of the treatment, see her looking weak or worried. Though the cheerfulness was bad, that would be so much worse.

"If you're sure, love? It would be nice to have the company."

Not once had Mum asked her to come too. She'd not even dropped the tiniest hint. There had been no need, as deep down Veronica knew that's what Mum needed and what she really should have done. Veronica had known and hidden away at work.

Mum chattered brightly all the way to the hospital. Veronica didn't join in but she did at least stop herself from snapping at her mother in the way she usually did when Sally was in full cheery flow. She almost smiled when Mum stayed positive as first a broken down delivery lorry delayed them and then they had trouble finding the correct department.

"We won't have to wait long at any rate," Mum said.

She was right. They'd not even had time to see if there

were any magazines worth reading when her name was called.

"Should I come in?" Veronica asked.

"No love. You wait here, I won't be long."

It wasn't until Mum had followed the nurse out that Veronica spotted someone she recognised: Sally. Glancing round, Veronica noticed the modern looking TV and the fancy coffee machine. So this was where Sally spent so much of her time. For once Veronica could do with someone who'd talk non stop about all kinds of happy things and distract her from reality. She knew Sally would be good at that and approached her colleague.

"Would you mind if I joined you?"

"That would be lovely!"

Veronica sat. She tried to think of something positive to say. "At least we didn't have long to wait."

"That was lucky, it can be a bit boring out here."

Before Veronica had properly registered that Sally had said something vaguely negative, she continued, "Is it your Mum, Veronica? How is she doing or would you rather not talk about it?"

"Yes, my Mum. Apparently she's doing really well, but I'd rather not talk about it if … um."

"Yes, absolutely. I understand," Sally said.

Veronica thought that perhaps, at last, she did.

"Soooo, Benedict Cumberbatch or Aiden Turner?"

"Sorry?" Veronica asked.

"Obviously they're both going to fancy you like crazy, but I'm only letting you chose one, otherwise it's not fair on the rest of us."

"Um, well I'd have to get to know them both really well before I could make an informed decision."

"Sensible girl. And you'd probably need to, er interview a few others too, sort of for control purposes," Sally said. "Tom Hiddleston perhaps and Zac Efron?"

"Oh yes and test them out in a variety of situations. On a beach, skiing, at a fancy party, driving fast cars obviously."

"Obviously."

The two girls chatted and giggled as they decided who else they'd audition and what kind of tests the men would be subjected to. It seemed hardly any time before Mum was walking towards them and another name was called. It wasn't until Sally stood up, that Veronica realised the next appointment was hers.

"It's been nice talking to you, Veronica. Thanks," she said and then hurried to join the waiting nurse.

Sally was a patient? That annoyingly cheerful manner had been her way of coping with her illness and treatment …and Veronica had refused to listen to a word of it. Worse than that, she'd withdrawn the friendship they'd begun to share about the time Sally must have had her first suspicions something was wrong. That must have hurt…

"Everything OK, love?" Mum asked.

"Shouldn't I be asking you that?" She never had, and with Mum she didn't even have the excuse of not knowing there was anything wrong.

"I'm fine. Although glad that's over for a while and we can get out of here."

"Actually, would you mind waiting just a bit longer? If you're not too tired? A girl from work has just gone in and she doesn't have anyone with her. I'd like to offer her a lift home, see she's all right."

"Of course, that's fine. I'm never too tired to sit still!" She settled herself next to Veronica. "I remember you telling me about a nice girl who helped you when you first got the job. Is that her?"

"Yes. Her name's Sally and she is nice. Unlike me. Mum, I'm so sorry I've let you go through this on your own. I didn't realise …"

Mum put her hand over Veronica's. "I know, love. We've both been in denial in our own way. Me by being as jolly as possible and you by pretending it wasn't happening."

"I can't pretend any more."

"No. So this friend of yours, where does she live?"

"She's not my friend, at least not yet. I hope she will be. She lives… actually I'm not sure where she lives but there's a nice teashop near there apparently. Maybe we could all try it together?"

"That will make a nice change."

"Yes, Mum, it will." The first of many, Veronica hoped.

18. Taking Steps

"Will you do it with me, Grandma?" Josh asks.

I'm not sure how much help I'll be when it comes to the homework of a ten-year-old boy, but I don't hesitate. "Of course I will, love," I reply as I grab hold of my frame and haul myself up.

Sometimes it's not about knowing the answers, or being able to do anything, it's just about being there by the other person's side.

His parents seem a bit surprised by my quick response but they shouldn't be. I'd made a promise to Josh when he was born that I'd always help him, always be on his side. A promise is still a promise, isn't it, even when the person you made it to can't remember?

You know when babies are expected and people say things like 'as long as it's healthy we don't care about anything else' and 'he's got all his fingers and toes'? Well Josh was born healthy and had all his fingers and toes. The toes were far smaller than the fingers though and the legs barely there at all. That's why I felt so protective of him, I suppose.

Not that I thought for a moment the other members of his family wouldn't love him. They're not like that at all. They treat me like one of their own. Josh calls me Grandma and so does his mum. In truth I'm no such thing, not even a step-Grandma, as Josh's great-grandfather and I never married. Caused all kinds of scandal in the village when I, half his age, moved in with him. Half his age and the only black woman some of them had ever met. Some of the neighbours only spoke to us so they could make snide little comments and collect gossip to spread.

My love's children weren't like that. Maybe it did take them a little time to adjust, but they were always polite. Pretty soon I think they realised how happy he was and decided that was the important thing. They were also grateful for the way I cared for him as his strength deteriorated. Long before that though, their children; Josh's mum and her siblings and cousins, were all calling me Grandma.

When my love died his family could have turned me out of my home, or at least tried. I'm not sure what the legalities were but I'm positive it never occurred to them that I shouldn't stay right where I was, as one of the family.

As I'd predicted, it was the same with Josh. They didn't love him any less because he was a bit different. He was family and that was that.

Of course he needed a little extra help with some things. Living on the seventh floor wasn't ideal so he, his sister and parents moved into this big old house with me. That's the best change there's been since I moved in myself.

I shuffle, one slow step at a time, towards Josh. His parents are definitely exchanging looks and shrugs. My skirt isn't tucked up showing my nickers; Josh's mum would just tug it back down if it was. My dinner isn't down my front and I have my teeth in. What then?

They've been concerned for me since my hip replacement I know. Poor loves, I gave them a bit of a scare by having a fall in town soon afterwards. Everything is fine now though. They've been encouraging me to go out.

"Come and see what we've done in the yard," Josh's dad said.

I admired it from the window.

"How about treating me to tea and cake in town?" my not really step-granddaughter suggested.

"I was planning to teach Josh to bake cookies," I countered. I did too and very nice they were.

I reach Josh and ease myself down onto the sofa next to him. I'd not expected to know the answers to the questions his teacher had set, but I had been expecting him to be looking at a text book. Instead he holds a leaflet for a sponsored walk. Quite a long walk, outside, and which I realise I've just agreed to take part in.

I look up at Josh's parents. They've been trying to get me to step outside the house for quite a time. They'd hinted and cajoled, tempted and nagged. Not once have they attempted to trick or blackmail me though. They could have done easily, just by saying it's what Josh wanted. Josh wouldn't trick me either.

"You really want to do this?" I ask Josh.

"Yes, Grandma. It's to raise money for the swimming pool at school and all my friends are doing it."

"It's quite a long way, love. It would take us a long time."

"That's OK, it isn't a race."

No, it wasn't. For this walk we could take tiny, tentative steps. The kind of careful steps Josh's family had never taken around me and which I'd never needed make in order to be accepted by them.

I can't refuse to make them now I've made a promise to Josh that I'll do it with him. An unwitting one maybe, but a promise is a promise.

"Help me up then, I'm going to need to practise a bit first," I say.

Josh's parents grin at each other.

"Don't know what you two are smiling at, this is going to cost you an absolute fortune in sponsorship money," I warn as, with Josh by my side, I step out into the sunshine.

19. Blowing Bubbles

A soap bubble floated down the crowded High Street and into Sara's line of vision. She raised a hand and batted it away. Her thoughts, as so often the case, were on Kayla. Until recently those thoughts had usually been happy ones, full of pride for her clever, caring and funny daughter. Now Sara was worried, and cross, about the change in the teenager.

Kayla used to spend several evenings a week studying her college text books and completing her course work. Now she went out drinking most nights. Sara had no idea if she was working at all. Worse than that, she never told her mother where she was going and Sara's only indication of when she'd return was hearing the commotion as she tripped up the steps to their flat and disturbed the neighbours in the early hours.

Two days ago Sara tried to reason with the girl, put her back on the right path, but her concern had got lost under the easier to express anger at loss of both sleep and good relationships with the people living close by. They'd argued. Again. The pair of them hadn't exchanged a single word since.

More bubbles drifted Sara's way and she instinctively swiped them away to make sure they didn't reach her eyes. Then she began to swat them on purpose – not just those which would have touched her face, but any which came near. They were easy to pop and doing so released a little of her tension.

A man smiled at her as she lunged for one which was almost out of reach. It must look odd, a grown woman chasing bubbles, but she swiped at another. She missed it, but not the grin on his face as he attempted to reach it himself. This time she returned the smile before continuing on her way.

Kayla's bad behaviour was just natural teenage rebellion, she knew. Sara had gone through a similar phase herself. It had ended, and so would the problem with Kayla if Sara was patient, or found a way to help.

Another flurry of bubbles filled the crowded street. There was no indication of where they'd come from and she was pleased others noticed them too. Without that she might have thought she was imagining them.

Instead of destroying the shiny bubbles Sara watched them float by. They were beautiful, like spherical rainbows, each an echo of the other. They tickled at a memory. Of course they did, she'd seen bubbles before, almost certainly blown them as a child, although she couldn't recall doing so.

She was reminded too of her necklace of crystal beads. Shiny, colourful and delicate, just like a stream of bubbles. It too sparkled in the light, reflecting every colour of the rainbow. Sara hadn't worn it in a long time.

Not since she'd become a single parent. At first she'd simply not had the opportunity to go anywhere it seemed appropriate to wear it. The necklace had been put away and almost forgotten – just like the fun, carefree side to Sara's personality.

More people stopped to look at the bubbles. Some trying to pop or even catch one, others just enjoying the brief spectacle. Where were they coming from? They seemed to hang in the breeze, playing with the currents and impossible to ignore.

A few steps on she spotted a man, sitting on a bench wearing dark glasses and holding a small bottle. As she watched, he withdrew something from it and blew a burst of bubbles into the air. As he raised a thumb up from the bottle's neck to guide the wand back in, rather than glancing down to see where it should go, she guessed he was blind. A white stick under the bench confirmed that, though she hadn't noticed it until she thought to look.

Entranced by the bubbles dancing around, she asked, "Do you mind if I sit here?"

"Not at all." He raised the bottle in her direction. "Would you like a go?"

"No, no. I just wondered why you were doing it."

"Would you have stopped to talk to me otherwise?"

Sara shook her head. Although the gesture wasn't any use to him, her silence seemed to provide the answer.

"That's one reason. The other is that people will sometimes describe them to me. If they're good at that, for a moment I see them too." He blew another long stream of bubbles. "How do they look?"

"Like rainbows," Sara said.

"I've never seen a rainbow, so you'll have to do better than that."

"Sorry…" He hadn't seen her necklace either so that comparison would tell him nothing. She needed to use senses other than sight.

"They're like a drink sparkling and popping on your tongue."

He grinned. "People who see them are drinking virtual

champagne?"

"No, not quite."

"A beer?"

"No, they're not at all bitter. Nor sickly sweet like cola… More like the fizz of a gin and tonic shared with a friend you've not seen in a while." She really should give Liz a ring and see if she fancied doing that.

He smiled and dipped the wand again. "I'll try and get ice and lemon into the next lot."

"Please, can I have a go?" a small boy asked.

His mother apologised and told him not to bother the man.

"I said please!" he defended himself.

The mother glanced at Sara, who gave what she hoped was an understanding and sympathetic smile.

Kayla had been the same at that age, ever eager to dive into an opportunity to have fun without stopping to consider any consequences or that she might be breaking any rules. Perhaps she hadn't changed so very much?

"He's welcome to a try if he'd like," the blind man said.

"Thank you. He's been chasing after them for a while, trying to work out where they came from."

The blind man held up the wand.

The child took a deep breath and blew as hard as he could. The liquid was swept from the wand, but no bubbles formed.

"Oh."

"You need to do it gently." He dipped the wand and held it out again.

The boy blew a couple of bubbles. There would have

been more, but he stopped to laugh. On each try he blew more until at last he produced a great stream of them, just as the blind man did.

"How do they look?"

"Like flying dinosaur eggs, ready to hatch!"

"No, like planets in a far, far away galaxy," another child declared.

For a while there was a small crowd of people, each taking a turn to blow bubbles and attempting to describe them to the blind man. Gradually, like the tiny orbs themselves, everyone but Sara drifted away.

"I would like to try now, if you don't mind?" she said.

The man handed her the bottle. "Go on then."

It didn't take Sara long to become proficient at filling the air with bubbles. How much easier for her than for him, as she could see the results of her efforts and know which technique was most successful.

"How do they look?" the blind man asked.

"Right now they're the sparkle in a girl's eyes when she tries on the perfect prom dress," Sara said, remembering Kayla's end of school prom. "But when they spread out they'll be like a baby's giggle. You don't always know what caused it, have no idea when it will return, but it's a tiny moment of joy you never quite forget." Again she was recalling her beloved daughter.

"Moments of joy? Are my bubbles really that?"

She told him how they'd lightened her dark mood of half an hour previously and how they seemed to do the same for others, how she'd exchanged smiles with strangers and although she hadn't worked out the answer to what was bothering her, she'd at least begun to think there could be a solution. As she spoke, she realised the blind man had given her his little bottle.

"You keep it, create more moments of joy," he said when she attempted to return it.

"Don't you want to blow more bubbles?"

"Yes and I will, but I want you to blow them too."

Sara thanked him and returned to work. The bottle stayed in her coat pocket until she poured herself a drink that evening. Nothing alcoholic as she was trying to set a good example for Kayla. Mineral water wasn't a lot of fun at the best of times, but worse when it was flat. What she needed was some bubbles.

She fetched the bottle from her coat in the hallway and began blowing them across the kitchen. She remembered the smiley man who'd laughed with her as they tried to pop a few. Perhaps she'd see him again tomorrow? And she really should give Liz a ring – when she'd mentioned the gin and tonic earlier it wasn't the drink she missed, but the reason to indulge.

There were other things Sara missed, such as the smile on Kayla's face. She was sure it would be back, but could hardly bear to wait for nature to take its course and return her beloved child to her. It was there again, the tickle to her memory. Mum said once that she'd felt like she'd lost Sara. That was a long time ago, when she'd been about Kayla's age.

Although she'd known Liz since preschool, Sara practically abandoned her to join a group who seemed much more exciting. They really had been, but in a dangerous way. She'd returned home one day, smelling of the cigarettes she'd shoplifted and ready with an angry response to the lecture she'd expected from her mother.

Instead of laying down the law, Mum had handed her the crystal necklace Sara had loved since she was a little girl, and been told would one day be hers. Mum wore it at Christmas and any occasions she could convince herself were special enough to warrant such shining beauty. Sara had worn it herself once; Mum lent it to her when she was a bridesmaid.

For a moment she'd greedily handled the iridescent crystals, hers to keep. Then doubts crept in. "What's going on, Mum?" she'd asked. "Why are you giving me this now?"

"You told me you're not a child anymore. I'm sure you're grown up enough to take good care of it."

"You're not ill, are you?"

Mum had smiled, making Sara realise she'd seen only a worried frown for some time. "No, love. I'm fine. Now, what are you doing tonight, going out with your new friends?"

"Dunno." That had been her plan, but she wanted to wear the necklace. She couldn't, not with them. They'd have laughed at it, or told her to sell it, or one of them would have taken it for themselves. As she thought that, she realised they weren't true friends. Not like Liz.

If she were to visit her, wearing the necklace, Liz wouldn't be so jealous at her having something nice that she'd mock her, nor would she be unable to see beyond its monetary value and suggest she part with it. Quite possibly she'd like to wear it herself, but she'd politely ask to borrow it and return it promptly.

Sara hadn't worn the necklace that night and hadn't gone out with friends old or new. Instead she'd talked to Mum. They'd had their differences since, and Sara made other mistakes, but things had been much better since then, both between them and in Sara's behaviour and prospects. Could history repeat?

The necklace was upstairs in her jewellery box and would be Kayla's one day. Not yet though. The clasp had become loose and the string holding the beads wasn't as secure as it once was. One clumsy movement and it would break. Before she handed it over, Sara would get it fixed.

The delay wouldn't matter. It wasn't the necklace which had made the difference back then. That was just the catalyst to halt their angry exchanges long enough for them to see that beneath the bad behaviour and angry words were two people who cared about each other very much.

Kayla came in, slamming the door as usual and charging straight upstairs so she could pretend not to hear Sara calling her. This time though her footsteps slowed, then resumed, but growing closer not further away.

"Mum, what's going on?" she called. "There's bubbles everywhere."

By way of reply, Sara blew more.

"Mum! What are you doing?"

"Blowing bubbles."

"Duh! I can see that."

"What else do you see?"

"You acting like a kid?"

"I mean the bubbles. How do they look?"

At first it seemed she wouldn't answer, but Sara blew more and looked at them instead of her daughter.

Kayla spoke quietly, the earlier sarcasm completely gone from her voice. "Like the bubbles you try to keep us in. Me like a little kid who can't be let out of your sight and you…"

"Go on, it's OK."

"You act like you have to be the perfect role model. You just work and look after me and have no fun at all. You aren't any fun and it's like I have to do everything right or your life means nothing. The pressure's too much sometimes, you know?"

"Oh, I…"

"Sorry, Mum. I didn't mean it like that. It's just… you are a bit boring lately." She squeezed Sara's hand, which both helped and made it worse.

Sara took out her mobile and sent Liz a text, G&T Saturday?

Kayla read it over her shoulder. "That's a bit more like it."

"I was thinking of giving you my necklace."

"The crystals? Mum it's lovely, but…"

"Yes, there is a but. I was going to give it to you now, but I've decided to hold onto it for a while and wear it myself a few more times. If I put my mind to it, I'm sure I'll be able to engineer a few special occasions."

"Go, Mum! You know, you look happier already."

"That's because I've had a moment of joy."

"Did you say joy or gin?"

"Funny you should say that." She told Kayla about the blind man and the various descriptions of his bubbles.

Kayla said, "They look like the inside of seashells when they're still wet from the sea… or how it used to feel to bring home a good school report and know how proud you'd be." She waved her hand in the air. "But they've all gone now."

Sara handed her the bottle. "Then blow some more."

At her first try, all Kayla managed to do was drip the liquid down her arm onto the kitchen table and make a noise like a deflating balloon.

She tried again and got better with each attempt. They looked like baubles on a Christmas tree, lights at the funfair, butterflies dancing by so prettily you'd almost swear fairies were real. Like ice just before a thaw, the fizz of optimism. Like hope and love and tiny moments of joy.

20. Can I Help?

"Stand back, everyone," Emma said.

Her trio of assistants moved well away from the oven. Emma pulled the door open a little way, allowing a waft of delicious smelling steam to escape, before opening it fully. She basted the roasting meat and turned the potatoes. Both were already looking close to ready. Her mouth watered. She'd not cooked a proper Sunday dinner in a long time. There just hadn't been time.

Her girls were at school now, but the youngest only went mornings, so dropping them off and going back twice in the day to collect them took up almost as much time as they spent in lessons. Then there had been Mum's new hip. The operation had gone well. So had the alterations to her flat; a higher toilet seat, shower cubicle where the bath had been, and a new armchair. That meant she'd be able to cope just fine on her own once she felt ready for that. Arranging it all, and the visiting in hospital, had taken a lot of Emma's time though.

"Can I help, Mum?" a little voice asked.

"Thanks, love." Emma gave her eldest the carrots and showed her how to use the peeler. It would have been quicker to do the job herself but she knew the girls loved helping her. It built up their confidence and they'd learn to actually be useful in time.

Next Emma whisked up Yorkshire pudding batter and put it in the fridge, just like her mum had taught her. Then, unlike she'd been taught, she opened a tin of rice pudding to use for the Queen of Puddings dessert she had planned and began spooning it into a dish.

"Can I help?"

"Yes, love, fetch me an egg will you, please."

"All gone, Mummy."

"There's a new box in the fridge."

After some rummaging, Emma heard, "Can't find it."

Just as she put down the tin and spoon she remembered. "Oh that's right. We had scrambled eggs for tea last night." Now what was she going to do for dessert? Queen of puddings without the meringue topping was just rice and jam; perfectly OK but not what they'd all been looking forward to.

"I could go to the shop and buy more."

It was on the tip of Emma's tongue to say no, but she stopped herself. She remembered going to the shop for Mum when she was little, and how proud she'd felt to be trusted and useful. It was so important for people to feel that, no matter what their age.

Eggs were eggs, it would be very hard to get the job wrong. The shop wasn't far away. If Emma walked there by herself it took less than five minutes. Her would-be helper wouldn't do it quite so quickly, but she'd get there and back in time for the pudding to be hastily assembled and put in the oven to brown whilst they ate the main course. Running the errand would really be useful too.

"I do know not to talk to strangers."

Emma grinned. "I know you do."

Of course she did. It was something Emma had learned from her mum and passed on to her kids. Should Emma let her go?

Eyes, almost the mirror of hers, pleaded that she should.

"And I know how to get there."

She should do as they'd all walked down there quite often, the last time being just the day before. Emma had held her hand then though. Letting her go alone was so different and naturally Emma felt responsible for her. But she knew she could walk that far, eggs weren't too heavy for her to carry and she should be able to complete the task without difficulty. There wasn't even a road to cross.

"Please let me. I'm going to have to learn to do things for myself sometime you know."

"Learn? You're the one who taught me. Thanks, Mum if you don't mind going it'll be a help."

21. Where Do Babies Come From?

After my sister gave birth to her daughter, Natalie, we had a serious talk. Not 'that' one – I knew the facts by then and clearly Ashley had put them into practice.

"I'm going to tell her the truth about everything, Nicole. Not skirt round difficult subjects like Nan did," Ashley said.

"Good idea," I agreed.

"Promise you'll do the same?"

I often looked after my niece and always kept that promise. You can imagine how surprised I was when she told me her goldfish had got bored of his bowl. "He's swimming in the sea now, Aunty Nicole."

Obviously it was dead. The salt water would do it even if it had been alive when my sister flushed it down the loo, which I guessed she had. I didn't say anything to little Natalie, but did have a few words with my sister.

"Remember what you said about telling her the truth?"

"I meant to, but when she saw the empty bowl she assumed he was in the sea. She probably got the idea from a cartoon. I didn't have the heart to put her right."

Lies told to children often are well meant. When I was five, Nan collected us from school. She explained Mummy and Daddy had gone for a drive in the car and not come back yet, so we were going to her house. Later she told us Mummy and Daddy were in heaven watching over us. "You'll both be living with me from now on."

We developed a crick in our necks scanning the sky for a glimpse of our parents. Between us we bumped into a lamp post, tripped over uneven paving and got tangled in a dog lead that week.

A teacher, noticing our bruises, had a talk with Nan. Afterwards we learned that although Mummy and Daddy were still watching over us and loved us very much, we wouldn't be able to see them doing it.

Ashley and I missed our parents, but Nan was lovely and very good at telling stories.

"Someone has annoyed the clouds," she'd say during a thunderstorm. "Birds probably. They tell them they look like silly things, or land on them and tickle them with their feet and they grumble about it."

With each crash she'd have us giggling at the funny names birds called clouds. Well, it wasn't the names so much which made us laugh, as her trying to form her plump, middle-aged body into the appropriate shape. Cotton wool donkey, upside down sheep and messy meringue certainly diverted us from the claps of thunder.

One day we were looking through photo albums and I noticed Mummy only had one child in some.

"You weren't born yet," Nan explained. That somehow led on to 'that' talk.

After the bit about the mummy and daddy loving each other very much and getting married, the whole thing seemed to be upsetting Nan so much I turned the page and asked why Mummy was wearing a small British flag. At the time I thought Nan made up The Spice Girls too.

Soon afterwards, a person down the road got very fat. She wasn't a lady; one of Nan's friends had said that. What she was, was a disgrace.

"We shouldn't judge," Nan said. "There may be things we don't know."

Ashley and I didn't know anything at all about her, except she wasn't married. When 'the disgrace' was seen with a baby I'm afraid we did judge her. As we 'knew' only married ladies had babies we decided she'd stolen it. Perhaps if we hadn't seen the two police officers so soon after making that deduction, things would have been a lot less embarrassing all round. 'That' talk from Nan was always going to be awkward, but having to repeat it, aided and abetted by a well meaning lady police officer, was totally excruciating.

Perhaps, now you know the background, you'll understand my reaction when little Natalie asked, "How did the baby get in Mummy's tummy?"

My pregnant sister was holding a coffee morning for her colleagues, which is why my niece was with me. I only panicked for a moment before noticing the way her question was phrased gave me a possible way to avoid 'that' talk.

"The baby isn't in her tummy, love." I told Natalie about the special place mummies have inside of them for growing babies, called a womb.

She accepted that but still had questions, including how the baby got into the womb and how it would get out again. The promise I'd made to my sister about telling her daughter the truth seemed to be ringing in my ears and almost drowned out Natalie's third question.

"Sorry, Natalie, did you say 'tooth fairy' just then?"

"Yes, look." She wobbled a loose tooth. "When it falls out the tooth fairy will buy it from me to give to the baby."

"Did Mummy tell you that?"

I learned my sister had promised Natalie the tooth fairy

would leave pennies under her pillow, but Natalie herself had guessed why she bought them.

"The fairy wouldn't want them for herself, they'd be too big," Natalie reasoned.

"Good point. Now, about the babies… you know I'm not married?"

Nicole nodded.

"Well, that means I don't know very much about making babies, so you'll need to ask Mummy. In fact, I think we should go to see her right now."

Knowing Ashley's work friends would be there, helping her out, would just add to the fun – for me at least.

22. Do Not Disturb

Reading glasses on, feet up, book open. I flip past the copyright notice and information that the author couldn't have written the story without the support of her family, turn the page and then it begins…

"Mum, I need a lift into town."

"Need?" I ask.

"Yeah. I'm meeting Suzy and we're going shopping. You know I need new shoes."

No doubt she does, plus cash from the bank of Mum and Dad to pay for them. Still, I actually get to talk to my daughter on the way and she does thank me when I drop her off by the mall. Plus the house will be quieter with her out of it. Am I a bad mother to think like that?

Home again, I head through the scuffed hallway to the lounge.

Reading glasses on, feet up, book open. The novel's first paragraph describes a cocktail bar in which…

"There you are," my husband says, as though calls on Mum's taxi service are unusual. "I'm famished."

"I'll call you when it's ready."

He's as capable as me of preparing a snack, but his hands are far dirtier and his overalls are leaving greasy streaks on the door frame. I make cheese on toast for three. It's soon gone, as is my son's brief appearance.

"Thanks, love," my husband says over the thumping bass

from above. "I needed that." Then he's back out to his shed.

I'm tempted to join him. There would be room surely for me to sit in a corner with my book? Perhaps, but it's cold out there and smells of engine oil. And he's got a music player too. If he switches it off, he'll explain what those pieces of metal will one day become.

Ear plugs in, reading glasses on, feet up, book open. I learn the heroine's name and then…

"Mum, I need my jacket for tonight."

"Which one?" I ask, but of course it'll be the one which needs washing, or ironing, or a button sewn on.

My brother rings as I'm waiting for him to fetch it. "Sis, I'm so glad I caught you. I need to ask a favour."

Of course he does. He really does.

I have all I need and I'm grateful. Really I am, but… A few hours peace of a weekend, to read a chapter or two, oh how I want that. I'm not wishing for anything else. Well, maybe new wallpaper in the hallway. That would be nice, but we can't afford a decorator and it's not a job I can do myself.

Miraculously the spare button for my son's jacket is still in the tiny plastic bag attached to the lining. It doesn't take long to sew it on it, brush off whatever he spilled on the sleeve and remind him where we keep the iron. It takes a lot longer to show him which is the cool setting and how to use a pressing cloth so the material doesn't go shiny, but I'm hoping spending the time now is an investment for the future.

"Cheers, Mum," he says when it's as smooth as his easy charm. "You're a star."

My brother's crisis takes longer to sort out. The problem's

ongoing and, even with the professional help he's getting might never be fully resolved, but he's happier when he leaves.

Not so my daughter when she returns home. There are, apparently, no shoes in town that she could possibly wear in public. There were last week, but her allowance is monthly, so she couldn't buy them then.

"Why is it that things are everywhere until you need them and then they vanish?" she asks.

I ask myself that same question a couple of hours later. My husband was there putting his oily clothes in the washing machine when I needed to get to the oven. My son's bass throbbed as I tried to dish up on a table covered with my daughter's magazine and nail polish. They were all there to eat, but dispersed when it was time to wash up.

I'm getting an idea.

"This weekend, I thought we'd decorate the hallway," I say over Wednesday night tea. "If we all work together it won't take long to strip off the old paper, sand down the woodwork…"

"But, Mum, I still need to find shoes."

"I get so much homework."

"I was thinking of taking your brother fishing."

Excellent! A quiet house. No one needing a lift, or a meal, or counselling. No more reading half a paragraph at a time. It'll be reading glasses on, feet up, book open and staying open.

On Thursday there are half hearted promises to 'see what I can do' and heartfelt explanations of the right footwear being essential to avoid becoming a social outcast, a looming physics test and the powers of fresh air to help soothe a worried mind.

Saturday morning I hear the front door close; loudly. That's the first one gone. The others won't be far behind. Reading glasses on, feet up, book open.

"Have you got a sponge?" It's my brother's voice and I just stare at him.

"Sorry, did I make you jump? The front door crashed, so I thought you'd know I was here."

"I did hear it," I tell him. "Sponge?" I ask.

He grins. "Don't look at me like I'm mad." That's his little joke. I'm glad he's feeling up to making it, even if it's accompanied by an odd request.

"To soak the wallpaper. You lot are tackling the decorating this weekend?"

"I'm not sure…"

"Mum, where's the sandpaper?"

"I've got some in the shed. The brushes and everything are out there too," my husband answers the question I'd not been sure I'd heard correctly.

"Yes, it seems we are," I tell my brother.

Soon they're all hard at work. They don't really need me to help. They will need new wallpaper to hang. It will be my job to get it. Perhaps it will take me a long time to choose, but if I'm lucky and find some quickly, I'll spend an hour in the store's car park. Reading glasses on, seatbelt off, book open.

23. Lost Sparkle

I pressed the switch which notified my next patient I was ready for them and hastily finished typing the notes of the previous one.

"Come in," I called, giving what I always hope is a reassuring smile.

Fourteen-year-old Ryan sidled in, alone. He slouched in the chair, his dull gaze not meeting mine. He looked healthy enough, but so many problems don't show on the surface.

"What can I do for you?" I asked.

He shrugged, still not looking up.

"Are you worried about something?"

He nodded. "My mum."

She's also a patient of mine, but I couldn't tell him anything. Partly because of confidentiality rules, but also because I'd not seen her for some time. I could however discuss his own concerns.

"What seems to be the problem?" I asked.

"She keeps saying she's a rubbish mother, but she's not. When she's OK, she's brilliant and even when she feels bad she makes my dinner and irons my uniform…"

It took some coaxing, but gradually he described her symptoms; tiredness, inability to concentrate, loss of appetite. "I think she's depressed," he said.

I agreed with his diagnosis and got busy on the computer, checking her patient notes and finding advice leaflets. As the printer whirred, I recalled my first encounter with depression thirty years previously.

I'd known Granny wasn't well because she didn't do anything. When I'd gone to her house before, we always did interesting things. Going to the park to play on the swings and roundabout, to the shops to buy vegetables and make them into funny faces on our plates, for long walks in the woods looking for flowers and birds. Even when she sat in front of the TV with me Granny would be knitting or sewing on a button.

When she got ill I still went for visits, but other than making us both a simple meal if I complained of hunger, it seemed she hardly noticed I was there. She always had the TV on, but she wasn't doing anything, not even watching it. She didn't laugh at the cartoons, or switch off when scary stuff came on like she had previously.

I asked my parents what was wrong and they did their best to explain, but I was only six. I understood being ill could make a person sad, as having to stay in bed all day rather than going out to play was no fun, but couldn't grasp that depression was itself an illness.

When I next saw Granny, I asked her what was wrong and didn't let her fob me off with, "Oh don't fuss," the way she did when Mum tried to get her to go to the doctors, or eat a meal.

"I guess I've lost my sparkle, love," Granny said.

Once I knew what was wrong, I knew exactly how to fix the problem. Like I said, I was only six. These things aren't so simple after years of medical training.

"We'll find it, Granny," I promised her. It was only fair; after I'd lost Blue Bunny she helped me find him. It had taken ages and ages, but she didn't get cross or give up.

First I looked all round the house. I found lots of shiny things, but they weren't really lost and seeing them didn't make Granny better. It took some persuading to get her to come outside and search, but I was too young to go to the park or shops all by myself.

We went everywhere I could remember Granny taking me and did everything I could remember us doing together, in the hope that would reveal where the lost sparkle was hiding. Gradually, instead of going along with the search because giving in to my enthusiasm was easier than thinking of reasons to stay indoors, staring unseeing at the TV, Granny began to join in.

"We could try the woods," she said one day. "We've not been there for a while."

Another day, when I dragged her round the shops, she bought some cauliflower and a tin of sweetcorn. For tea, instead of the plain sausage and blob of mashed potato she'd cooked me the week before, we made the meal into a snowman, with white curly hair and yellow teeth.

Some time after that, we saw a big puddle and Granny took my hand and we ran up to it and jumped right in. Mud went everywhere and Granny laughed.

"Are you better?" I asked.

"Yes, love. I feel much better than I did."

"Where did you find your sparkle?"

"Right here!" She poked me on the nose.

At first I though she meant in the mud which was splattered on my face and clothes.

"You, Rebecca. You're my sparkle."

"But I didn't get lost."

"No love, but when I was ill, I couldn't see you shining."

Back in the present, I took the leaflets from the printer and handed them to Ryan. I explained that recovery might be a long process and there was no magic cure, but being physically active and eating a balanced diet would help his mum. The leaflets gave advice on helping her achieve that, and included website addresses where he could get more information and support for them both.

"Can you talk to her?" he asked.

I'd seen from her notes she was overdue a routine check. I'd make sure she was reminded and, if she responded, the appointment would be with me, so I could talk about this, but there was no guarantee she'd come in.

"Only if she's willing to see me, Ryan. You can suggest that, but whether or not she agrees, you're already doing the most important thing. You're being you."

"It's not doing any good. I don't think she's really noticing me."

"Maybe not right now she isn't, but keep being there for her and showing you care and eventually it will make a difference, it really will."

"Thanks, Doc." He looked up and that dull hopeless look in his eyes had been replaced with a hint of sparkle. Helping his mum regain hers would take longer but I was confident that, between us, we'd do it.

24. Visiting Memory Lane

"Who are all these people?" Hayley asked.

Arabella peered at the faded photograph. "That was my mother, and this one is her sister. She would have been your great-great-grandmother." Arabella identified other family members. "And that one in the centre is me."

"Gosh, you were really pretty, Aunt Arabella."

"I was rather."

"Not that you aren't now," Hayley hurriedly added.

Arabella laughed. "Don't worry child, by seventy-nine one no longer hopes to be called pretty."

"OK maybe pretty isn't the exact word to describe you now, but you look great. Characterful – like a love-etched Dame Maggie Smith."

"That's such a nice thing to say."

"And you're so fit and active it's impossible to think of you as nearly eighty. Honestly I'm not just saying that, you really don't seem old."

"It's being around young things like you," Arabella said. It was probably true. When she was home, Arabella helped out in the charity shop for an hour or two at the busiest times. Students often visited in their lunch break and Arabella loved chatting to them as they searched for bargain clothes, fancy dress items or even things to help with college projects. Being on her feet the whole time might have been tiring without their infectious enthusiasm and energy.

Arabella enjoyed herself even more on her trips away. She was fortunate to often be invited to stay with different family members for a week or so at a time. Spending time with different people, all of whom were younger than her, stopped her getting in a rut. The same applied to the fun of travelling to see them. That involved trains or coaches, even a plane occasionally, sleeping in different beds and eating different foods.

"So, what was the occasion?" Hayley asked, interrupting her thoughts.

"Occasion?"

"For the party?" Hayley indicated the old photograph.

"Oh, probably no real occasion. Back then uncles, aunts and cousins would all come for picnics in the garden whenever the weather was nice, or the strawberries were ripe, or someone had discovered a new cake recipe. Everyone lived close by so it was easy to do that."

In her youth, Arabella's extended family spent a lot of time together and knew each other well. Now the only big gatherings were weddings and those were infrequent and without much chance to talk to anyone for very long.

"Things have changed a lot," Hayley said, sounding a little wistful.

"Indeed they have. I don't miss hauling wet laundry into the spinner, or lugging the carpets outside to beat the dust from them, I can tell you. And it's so easy now to share news and pictures, no matter how far away people are."

"Yeah, some things are better. Not the clothes though." Hayley, who studied textiles, indicated the summer frocks and hats on show in several photos, making Arabella feel rather pleased she always took the trouble to dress nicely, even to go food shopping.

"I bet there are other things you miss too, like these family gatherings?" Hayley said.

Arabella nodded. It was a shame it was no longer possible to get all the family together. "People seem so busy now." They really were, despite all the labour saving devices they crammed into their tiny homes. Gardens were smaller too, so any group event required hiring a hall or other venue. Even then difficulties arose as they lived so far apart. Still, Arabella had no call to complain. She was very fortunate to see them all from time to time, and everyone was very good to her.

Arabella understood free time was precious in a way it hadn't been in her youth. She didn't blame her relatives for always wanting to be doing things when she visited. Besides, the places they took her to were often interesting. Her only regret was they never really talked to her beyond enquiries into her comfort, updating her on news and sharing plans for the day ahead.

Arabella continued telling her grand-niece about family gatherings of the past and mentally added 'the old days' to her list of things people talked to her about. Hayley, and one or two others, were interested in family history and made time to ask a few questions.

Soon there was a new topic of conversation; enquiries into what Arabella would like for her birthday.

"Pretty cards would be lovely, but no gifts, please," she said as she did every year. There was truly nothing she needed or even wanted, at least nothing which could be wrapped.

"But it's your eightieth, that's a bit special."

Arabella considered requesting a family gathering. Something where she could see them all together and really talk to them properly. It was far too late to organise it now though. Unlike in times gone by, you couldn't just announce you'd be at home to visitors on a certain day and expect a houseful. Besides it would be so expensive for most of them, with the travelling and hotels and many would have to take time off work. She couldn't ask it. Well, not precisely.

"What I'd really like is to see some of you, as many as possible, and to sit down and talk. Could it be done on a computer?"

Arabella was told that in theory it could, but even then getting everyone involved would be difficult. Her great-nephew Derek was overseeing some kind of project he'd organised, Lucy and Matt had a holiday booked, Lilibeth had an article to research, even Hayley had plans for most of the day.

"Mum and Dad promise to take part," Hayley said. "Cousin Stephen will and some others and I'll definitely get online sometime."

"That will be nice," Arabella said. It would. Of course she'd have loved to see everyone on her birthday, but chatting to a few of her relations was a lot better than nothing. Even nicer, as she had no computer herself, someone would need to bring one and help her work it. Whoever that was would be there to have a proper conversation with, between the virtual chats.

Hayley phoned to break the news a week before Arabella's birthday. "We've arranged a surprise for your birthday, Aunt Arabella, but we've realised we'll have to tell you so you can pack."

"I'm coming to stay again so soon? Oh, that's lovely."

"Um, no. The family have all put in the money for a week's coach trip for you, the week of your birthday."

"Oh."

"I won't give you all the details as we do want you to have a bit of a surprise."

"No, of course."

"That is, OK? You do enjoy travelling…"

"Oh, yes. It's very generous of you all. Thank you."

"You'll need a lift to the pick-up point of course. I could drive you, if you like."

Arabella reminded herself that although Hayley still seemed so young, she was a competent driver who'd earned her licence over a year ago. "That's kind of you, but it's a very long way for you to come. Perhaps a taxi might be better?"

"I was thinking, if it's all right with you, I might come down the day before and stay with you for the night. You did promise to show me photos of Mum, when she was little."

"That would be wonderful, Hayley dear. Yes, please do that and we could have a meal at The Swan, my treat. I hear the new chef is very good."

Arabella hoped it wasn't obvious that her enthusiasm for Hayley's company was considerably greater than for the coach trip. It was a kind thought of her family and she was sure she'd enjoy it.

In a way it was quite exciting to not know where she would be going, especially as she was sure to be well looked after wherever it was. There would be meals cooked for her and she was certain the destinations would be interesting. Better yet, sitting beside other people for an extended period almost always meant conversation. She would not let herself be disappointed her companions would be strangers. They wouldn't be after the first hour anyway, would they? Yes, Arabella was sure it would be wonderful. And she was fairly certain the family would arrange for cards to reach her on her birthday. Some of those were likely to contain snippets of news, so be almost as good as a chat.

When Hayley arrived she didn't just look at Arabella's photos. She brought with her a disc full of pictures of the family which Arabella could view on her television.

"That's so clever of you and these are easier for me to see than ordinary photographs."

"It's quite easy to do on the computer. I'll send you some more… um, a bit later. Now, do I have time for a shower before we go out tonight?"

"Definitely. And don't worry how long you take in the bathroom. I'm going to have a nap, just to make sure I have enough energy to last through to dessert."

"I like your priorities! What time do you want to set off?"

"I've booked the taxi for quarter past seven."

"There's no need for a taxi. I can drive us there."

"Yes, but not back again after I've plied you with champagne to get you to tell me where I'm going tomorrow."

"You can't make me talk, Aunt Arabella." Hayley mimed zipping her lips.

Hayley was wrong about that. She didn't divulge the destination, but the two of them talked all through the meal and on into the night once they were back at Arabella's.

At midnight Arabella said, "It's the day of the trip, you can tell me now where I'm going."

"All right then." Hayley took a piece of paper from her bag. "You're going to the Lake District, starting off in somewhere called Kirkby Stephen…"

"Oh, but that's…"

"Sedburgh," Hayley continued as though Arabella hadn't spoken. "Then Kendal, Winster Underbarrow, round some of the meres or waters or whatever they're called and over to Whitehaven…"

"Hayley! Show me that."

Hayley handed it over.

"But this seems incredible."

"It's not really so far."

"Not the distances I don't mean. I was born in Kirkby Stephen and I went to school here," she indicated one of the stops. "And later we moved there and during the war I worked at Whitehaven. Everywhere on this list means something to me."

"Does it really?"

"Santon Bridge is the place Hugh and I went walking when he got leave. It's where we shared our first kiss." There hadn't been many afterwards; his plane had been shot down a month later. That was somewhere else far away from the lakes though. She had only happy memories of the area she'd soon be viewing from air-conditioned luxury.

"You knew!" Arabella exclaimed. "That's why you chose it."

"I didn't know all of it, but you've talked about some of these places so I thought you'd like to go there and although

I may have dropped a few hints, it isn't all my fault. Uncle Derek had quite a bit to do with it and so did Lucy and Matt."

"What a wonderful family I have."

"I'm glad you said that. Now I'm off to bed, we have quite an early start tomorrow."

"Of course, my dear. Good night."

Arabella sat up for a little while longer, looking again through her photo albums. In a way she would be surrounded by family on her birthday, as she carried her memories with her.

She slept well that night, waking in time to prepare a good breakfast to set her up for the trip and sustain Hayley during her long drive home. After bacon, eggs and plenty of mushrooms, Hayley carried Arabella's case to her car and placed it against one of her own.

"Are you going away too?"

"Hmm."

"Where?"

"You couldn't make me talk with champagne, Aunt Arabella. You have no chance without."

"Tell me you're not eloping, child."

Hayley giggled. "I promise I'm not eloping!"

"What then? Trekking in Timbuktu?"

"No."

Arabella made a few even wilder guesses during the drive, but only succeeded in making Hayley laugh.

Hayley parked the car and unloaded Arabella's case.

"Can I help you with that, madam?" a man asked.

"Thank you. That's most ...Derek! What are you doing

here?" Arabella gasped.

"Hayley didn't let on about your surprise then? She is a one for keeping secrets."

"Actually she isn't. Two glasses of champagne and I got the truth from her."

"Actually, it was one cocktail, half a bottle of champagne and one liqueur coffee and I still didn't tell."

"Don't you remember, child? Kirkby Stephen, Whitehaven…"

"Cousin Stephen, Uncle Derek, Matt, Lucy," Hayley countered. "Mum, Dad, Lillibeth… all of us. We could only pick the whole itinerary if we booked the whole coach, so we're all coming with you."

"Don't worry, Aunt Arabella," Derek added. "I've brought more champagne, so you'll have no trouble getting us to talk."

Before they set off, the family posed for a group photograph. Arabella hoped that in about seventy years some yet to be born member of her family would look at it and ask, "Who are all these people, Aunt Hayley?"

Thank you for reading this book. I hope you enjoyed it. If you did, I'd really appreciate it if you could leave a short review on Amazon and/or Goodreads.

To learn more about my writing life, hear about new releases and get a free exclusive ebook, sign up to my newsletter – subscribepage.io/ItLSNa or you can find the link on my website patsycollins.co.uk

<u>More books by Patsy Collins</u>

Novels

Firestarter
Escape To The Country
A Year And A Day
Paint Me A Picture
Leave Nothing But Footprints

Little Mallow cosy mystery series

Disguised Murder and Community Spirit in Little Mallow
Dependable Friends and Deceitful Neighbours
in Little Mallow
Deadly Words and Innocent Gossip in Little Mallow

Non-fiction

From Story Idea To Reader
(co-written with Rosemary J. Kind)

A Year Of Ideas:
365 sets of writing prompts and exercises

Short story collections

Over The Garden Fence
Up The Garden Path
Through The Garden Gate
In The Garden Air
Beyond The Garden Wall

No Family Secrets
Can't Choose Your Family
Keep It In The Family
Family Feeling

All That Love Stuff
With Love And Kisses
Lots Of Love
Love Is The Answer

Slightly Spooky Stories I
Slightly Spooky Stories II
Slightly Spooky Stories III
Slightly Spooky Stories IV
Slightly Spooky Stories V

Just A Job
Perfect Timing
A Way With Words
Dressed To Impress
Coffee & Cake
Not A Drop To Drink
Making A Move
A Clean Bill Of Health
Your Good Health
Criminal Intent
Crime In Mind
Days To Remember